Saving One

A novel
by Steve Caplan

ISBN: 978-1-945917-12-7

Printed in the United States of America

Front Cover Photo: "Bench in the Park" by Vergo.me
Back Cover photo: Naava Naslavsky

Also by Steve Caplan:

Matter Over Mind
Welcome Home, Sir
A Degree of Betrayal

"Making other books jealous since 2004"

Big Table Publishing Company
Boston, MA
www.bigtablepublishing.com

Acknowledgments

As usual, I need to thank my family, Eylon, Mika, Naava and Ginger, for putting up with me when I go "off the grid" and into full writing mode. In addition, I am grateful that everyone at home is always willing to serve as a sounding board, both for new ideas, and experimentally to see if my ideas hold up on paper.

I also would like to thank my editor, Robin Stratton, at Big Table Publishing, for continually pushing me to improve my novels. Her exhaustive efforts to obtain the most compelling, exciting and believable story, her great eye for detail, and finally a superb sense of humor have made it a pleasure to produce my second novel with her at Big Table Publishing.

For my dad, who means so much to me

Chapter One

Jeffrey Coleman fumbled his Metro SmartTrip out of his pocket, slid through the turnstile and wearily followed the other passengers onto the escalator. As he saw the light at the end of the tunnel and prepared to emerge from the bowels of the Bethesda station, he felt his phone buzz in his pocket–not once, but three or four times–probably an accumulation of messages while he was underground and out of coverage. He swiftly pulled the device out of his pocket, but someone on his left jostled him, and the phone clattered onto the moving steps; he scrambled to recover it, sweating profusely as hurried commuters pushed their way past him. Finally a young woman who stood a few steps below handed him his phone. Thanking her sincerely, he glanced at the screen, frowning as an additional text came through. All from his son, Mark.

Jeffrey sighed, pocketed the phone, and wondered how he was going to get out of this mess. "I'm just not ready," he mumbled to himself. Then he tried, "You know I loved your mother very much, but I just don't feel comfortable making a public show." Nothing seemed to work very well, but before he could put together a solid defense, the phone rang.

"Hello?"

"Dad. I've been trying to reach you. It's getting really late–Friday is the second anniversary of Mom's passing, and you still haven't answered us on how we're going to commemorate her life."

Jeffrey shuddered and felt his eyes well up with tears. There was a bulge in his throat, and he didn't trust himself to speak. "Mark. I just...I, well. I can't do it."

There was silence on the other end of the line, and while Jeffrey felt compelled to fill that silence, he also felt that he had nothing further to say. Finally Mark said, "But Dad, you know how important this is to me. And Tamara. Can't we honor Mom's memory properly?"

"Mark, let me get back to you. I need to think about this; it's not easy for me."

"Come on, Dad. We've been discussing this for two months. You've got to let us know tonight. We can't do things at the last minute."

"Alright," Jeffrey answered. "Give me a few hours–I need to get home to Vi. I'll call you later."

"Don't forget!"

In January it would be two years since Annie had left him; not her fault–it was her messed-up Jewish Ashkenazi genes. Despite all of his contacts at the National Cancer Institute, no one had been able to help. "If we had caught it earlier," the oncologist said, "there might have been a chance. But once it's spread through the lymph nodes, it's really tough to control."

Yeah, thought Jeffrey, tough my ass. More accurately, impossible. What the hell was the point of being a biomedical researcher when he was helpless when it really mattered? He could publish the most exquisite papers on how proteins moved about through the cell, how mitochondria underwent fusion and fission– he could even visualize those processes in real time with fluorescence microscopy, watching movies that followed individual proteins as they cavorted and navigated through the depths of the cell. But when it came to actually doing something to relieve Annie's suffering–in real time–he was as clueless as any Wal*mart greeter, post office employee, or stupid politician. He made a mental note not to say that out loud–it wouldn't do for a government employee at the National Institutes of Health to bash the political echelon. But he felt himself succumbing again to misery; just a tax-spending scientist with his high-tech toys, feeding his own indulgent curiosity.

Jeffrey was well aware that his thoughts were blasphemous and went against everything that he had lived and fought for. He had modeled his philosophy of research on that of the late Nobel laureate, Dr. Arthur Kornberg: that basic and often serendipitous discoveries had historically led to the most significant medical advances in the 20th century. But in truth, his convictions had wavered considerably since Annie's death.

He knew that he was being unfair to himself, but he couldn't help it. His friend Ravi, who was a nephrologist at the NIH, had said, "But without you guys pushing the limits, figuring out how things work, would we even have new drugs to test?"

Jeffrey had replied, "But for all my publications, for all the beautiful molecular mechanisms my lab has elucidated in the last twenty years, has it led to a single new drug being tested? To a single life being saved?"

"Come on, Jeff. You know that's not how it works. You always give that great little talk about how antibiotics were discovered by accident. How so many times it's when science goes awry that great advances are made."

"Yeah, well. Maybe I should teach my students and post-docs to be more careless." There was more than just a hint of disillusionment in Jeffrey's voice. "Maybe my problem is that we're too calculated. Too good at what we do. Perhaps if we weren't so efficient at characterizing these mechanisms that we work on, if we were sloppier and not so good at what we do, we might find real treatments for cancer.

"Jeff, Jeff. Science is a big enterprise, and you are great at what you do. We need the thinkers and leaders like you. No one can do everything. You did everything that you possibly could. Give yourself a break."

Ravi was a true friend, but Jeffrey didn't feel any better after the conversation. What was it that everyone was telling him? Time— that's it. That only time will eventually dull the pain. He only hoped he would live that long.

Jeffrey Coleman unlocked his apartment door and braced for the onslaught. Sure enough, his young high-energy Vizsla-Labrador retriever was all over him before he could step inside. With great vertical leaps, she plastered his face with a series a wet kisses, licking his nose and eyes and almost knocking off his metal-framed glasses.

"Okay, Vi, okay, that's a girl, okay… " Flipping on the light, his eyes, fell as always, on the worn sofa and misshapen recliner in the living room, the few dishes resting on a towel by the sink, and the overall lack of coziness. The walls sported a few of his framed travel photographs, and with his son Mark's help he'd hung a large map of the world over the bookcase. Sparse on furnishings and decorations, but comfortable. Kicking the door closed with his foot and tossing his mail onto a small table, he crouched to favor his best friend with a serious rubbing session. Vi submitted, happily exposing her reddish-brown belly, paws raised in the air, as she groaned contentedly; all the while flicking her tongue at his face. "Good girl," he said, as if she had performed some notable achievement. Then, with a groan of his own, he got back to his feet, only to kick off his shoes and collapse on the couch. Vi promptly spread out beside him with her head firmly tucked in his lap, wet nose poking into his ribs. Personal space was not a concept with which she was familiar.

It was in some ways the hardest part of his day. Work in the lab was done, and there was no longer a need to keep up appearances. In other words, not only was his personal distraction of work at the lab and his office done for the day, but so was his interaction with the rest of the human race. Without post-docs, students and other trainees needing him in the lab, he was free to mourn and mope about in his little apartment. He would have worked 24/7, as he had in the good old days–just to avoid being alone with his thoughts and memories–but he was no longer a spring chicken, and his body complained when he tried.

Pushing himself up from the sofa with a Herculean effort, Jeffrey leashed Vi, exited his apartment, and headed down the flight of stairs with his exhilarated partner. As he allowed her time to do her business, punctuated by a few treats to reinforce her good behavior, he reflected on how it might be nice to be a dog. All one's needs taken care of, and life continually carefree and happy. After all, dogs were separated from their mothers early on in life, and for the most part, they were a congenial species, typically happy with their human family. And, he thought wistfully, even the idea of a partner wasn't an emotional commitment for a dog–just a biological need. Sighing heavily, he called to Vi and they plodded back up to the apartment.

He glanced at the clock-radio on top of the refrigerator: 7:30– time to think about dinner, and the main non-work-related decision of the day: wine or beer? Beer was filling, and he might eat less if he started out with a Sam Adams. But there was only one in the fridge.

Wine, on the other hand, sat beside the clock on top of the fridge in a three-liter box and wasn't likely to run out after a glass or so. With that decision having been made, he attended to Vi's kibble and pulled a container of green curry chicken takeaway from the freezer to thaw.

As the microwave warmed his dinner, he heard a *pop* inside, indicating that most likely now curry was splashed all over the inner walls of the oven. He had, of course, forgotten to cover the plate. "Ahhh, Jeesum Crow," he said. Mark had been on at him last week about invoking the name of Christ in his cursing. "Come on, Dad, it's not exactly politically correct to say 'Christ on a crutch.'"

"But nearly everybody says 'Chhhrist!'" Jeffrey had argued.

"Dad, but you're a Jew and you don't believe in Christ."

"Well, I don't believe in anything. If any God cared, Mom would be alive. Besides, Ravi and my Hindi friends also say 'Christ on a bike!'"

"Dad."

"All right," Jeffrey had promised. "I'll try to control my expletives."

Jeffrey sometimes forgot that he wasn't alone in his grief. Mark had been deeply attached to his mother, but he'd seen Jeffrey's misery and somehow managed to deal with his own sorrow while being there for his father. *That's another reason I'm such a failure,* Jeffrey thought. *I should be taking care of my son, and instead, he's looking after me.*

It had been Mark, together with his wife Tamara, who had cleared out Annie's closet and packed everything off to Goodwill. Annie had not been attuned to fashion and did not have an extensive wardrobe; nonetheless, they had removed over 25 boxes out of the old house. Jeffrey had been unable to face such a daunting task; he had barely been able to enter the bedroom to haul his own belongings out. Sleeping there was out of the question. Mark helped Jeffrey find an apartment in Bethesda within walking distance of the NIH, with a brand new and never slept-in bed, and most importantly, lacking any of the memories that haunted his father.

After three months of his dreary existence in his new, Spartan accommodations, Jeffrey was shocked one Saturday morning when Mark showed up with a beautiful auburn dog. As soon as she set eyes on Jeffrey, she bounded over with tail wagging, climbed up and put her paws on his shoulder, and gave him a big wet lick.

"She already loves you, Dad," Mark laughed.

"She *is* sweet," Jeffrey said, patting his new companion on the head. "But I can barely look after myself right now."

"I found her in a shelter—you'll be great for each other. You'll take care of her, and she'll take care of you. You'll see."

As it turned out, Mark was right. Those lonely hours when Jeffrey came home from work were now peppered with conversations with Vi. Sometimes she answered his questions, like when he asked if she wanted to go for a walk, with great vertical leaps in the air. Mostly, though, she listened patiently, and gently cocked her head when Jeffrey raised the pitch of his voice and came to a question of some sort. "Should I cook dinner or do take out?" Jeffrey could interpret the answer any way he liked. Having someone listen, someone attentive to him, did seem to relieve the loneliness.

No sooner had he gotten comfortable sat at the table with his wine, curry, and both Vi and the internet for company, than his cell phone chimed. Grumbling, he reached for it. "Crow on a crutch!" It had to be another one of those bloody telemarketers—who else would bother him at dinnertime? Mark had told him yesterday that he and Tamara were headed to visit friends in Richmond, and his social life had basically come to a standstill after Annie died. For sure, it was one of those brain-dead telemarketers. He answered, "It's done, but there's blood *everywhere*."

There was a long pause, then a worried but familiar voice said, "Uh, are you okay, Jeffrey?"

Embarrassed, Jeffrey used the full name of his post-doc. "Oh, Jairaj. I'm sorry." He didn't have the energy to try to explain his warped sense of humor to Jai, so he muttered, "I thought you were someone else." He picked up his fork. His stomach was beginning to rumble with the succulent curry at close range. "What's going on? Have you completed the experiment?"

Through a lot of hard work and tremendous persistence, Jai had developed a new model for understanding the biogenesis of mitochondria in cells and the lab team was racing to complete a series of experiments requested by the reviewers of the manuscript they had submitted three months ago. Two of the three reviewers had been very positive, and although they had asked for additional data, the experiments that they requested had been reasonable and truly would improve the manuscript. On the other hand, the third reviewer had been rather negative, and without explicitly bashing the paper, he–or she–had included a laundry list of experiments that would take the group at least a year to complete. And Jeffrey knew that these experiments weren't designed to improve the paper. They were merely a way for a reviewer to stall the Coleman group and delay or even prevent them from publishing.

From a meeting he had recently attended, Jeffrey knew that the Danfield lab at UCSF had similar data, and although Jeffrey was confident that his group was way ahead of Danfield's, by reputation he knew that his rival would do anything to publish first. *Am I being paranoid?* Jeffrey wondered. Well, "paranoid" wasn't the right word– you can't be paranoid about something that has a high probability of happening. "Seriously concerned" was more accurate. The problem was not merely that the Danfield group would reap all the credit–Jeffrey knew that if Danfield managed to publish ahead of them, the high-tier journal to which he and Jai had submitted their manuscript would drop their study like a hot potato. Yeah, it didn't matter that much to him–or at least he no longer cared as he once did–but this could make or break Jai's career, and Jeffrey wanted to support his loyal co-worker.

"Well," Jai admitted, "There is a bit of a problem."

Jeffrey didn't need a Ph.D. in psychology to sense his young colleague's reluctance to speak. "Out with it Jai, tell me what's going on."

"The experiment hasn't worked yet technically, but that's not why I'm calling."

"Go on."

"It's Sarala, my daughter. As you know, she has been serious about gymnastics for several years."

"Yes."

"Well, she has been invited to the US Olympic trials."

"Congratulations," Jeffrey said, not sure where the conversation was headed.

"Yes, but while this is good, it is also, ah, difficult."

"Sure," Jeffrey said. "I bet it's really competitive, and that's a lot of pressure for a 16-year old."

"No–I mean yes. It is a lot of pressure, but the problem is that the trials are in Seattle, and they are three weeks long."

Jeffrey toyed with his meal–the curry was no longer warm, and he'd have to nuke it again when he got off the phone. "So, Jai, it sounds like you'll be 'batchin' it like me for a while. I'll take you out for dinner, if you can finish those experiments."

"Thank you, Jeffrey, truly, but I will need to accompany Sarala; remember that Radha is now in medical school at Georgetown, and she can't take off time for this."

Jeffrey put down his fork, no longer even hungry. He had completely forgotten that Jai's wife was now a medical student. "You mean that you'll be gone for three weeks. Now?"

"I will make it up on nights and weekends. I promise to you. But I must let Sarala have this chance of a lifetime."

There goes the paper. How the hell will we beat the Danfield group if Jai is away for the next three weeks? "All right, Jai. Good luck to Sarala. We'll do what we can to keep things rolling in the meantime. But remember, it's your career on the line. I already have a permanent position and tenure."

"Thank you, Jeffrey. I will talk to Reg in the lab and ask him for some help."

Tossing the remains of his half-eaten dinner in the trash–the curry was too spicy for Vi–Jeffrey reflected for the hundredth time on how today's young scientists just didn't have the commitment that his generation did. And then, for the hundredth time, he thought about the nights and weekends that Jai had spent in the lab, and decided that today's scientists were just as dedicated, if not more so. But it didn't change the facts: they'd have to hurry if they were going to beat the Danfield lab to publishing.

Jai returned his cell phone to his pocket and went back into the kitchen. Although Radha had precious little time for cooking, she still managed to throw together some *Aloe Chole* once a week, and he was very hungry. In fact, his naturally big appetite, which had been on hold while he talked to Jeffrey on the phone, had now come back with a vengeance. He sat down between Sarala and his son Nadish, across the table from Radha, who glanced wistfully at the clock above the window.

"Well," Sarala asked. "What did your boss say?"

Jai stroked his trim moustache. "That if I go with you, he will fire me."

"Dad!" Sarala shouted. "Stop joking, and be serious for once—these are Olympic trials!"

Jai could see Radha shaking her head slowly—not in annoyance, but knowing that Jai always had to try to play some prank on his kids. They knew that, too—in fact they had come to expect it from him. He secretly suspected that if he failed to play some joke on them, and just answered a question directly, that they'd be worried that something happened to him. And they'd probably never believe him.

"Let's look for tickets to Seattle after dinner," he said. "I'll bring my laptop and do as much as I can from the hotel room."

"Was he surprised that you're going and not me?" Radha continued to feel pangs of guilt about her own retraining as a physician. She had received her Masters degree in science at the prestigious India Institute of Science in Delhi, but with the birth of her two children, and Jai's doctoral degree in the US followed by his competitive and exhausting post-doctoral position in DC, she had decided to work as a lab technician and not pursue a more ambitious career path. But once Sarala and Nadish were in high school, Radha had begun to feel that there must be more to her career than injecting mice with tumors and doing animal husbandry. Given her interest in healing, and her strong feelings of discomfort in not finding a female OB GYN to look after her during her pregnancies, she made up her mind that she would become an obstetrician.

"Yes," Jai answered. "He had forgotten you're at Georgetown now, but he'll get over it. I think he's mellowing in his middle age."

Mark stuffed his laptop into his backpack, grabbed his jacket, and left the lab. It was well past 8:30 in the evening; another twelve-plus hour day. With his intense dedication and commitment to hard work, and with his fellowship, he was on the fast track to success. At 29, he was one of the youngest post-docs to receive the Innovation Fellowship, and was beginning to put together his application for faculty positions. As he headed toward the Metro station, he wondered how much he owed to his father's career advice—not to mention his tendency to talk about science all throughout his childhood: at meals, in the car, and while Mark was brushing his teeth.

Tamara would actually be home this evening and for the rest of the night, having done a double shift at the hospital the previous day. Every time he felt like complaining about his long hours and unsuccessful experiments, he thought of Tamara, a registered nurse working on the pediatric oncology ward, and his frustration vanished. How on earth could she possibly deal with poor, sick kids all day long? Someone had to do it, but he was glad it wasn't him. It had to be heart-wrenching to see those brave, suffering kids. But he knew it was no picnic physically, either. Night shifts, double shifts, on her feet for hours at a time. Lifting kids and carrying them, holding them during treatments. He knew that he could never have the kind of strength required for that type of work. Angels' work.

Mark knew that neither he nor Tamara could sustain this kind of lifestyle much longer. It wasn't the physical demands that he worried about; he knew that with Tamara newly pregnant, things would have to change. They might be able to continue at their current pace for another six months—perhaps even nine months, until the baby was born. But after that? She would have to cut back on those double shifts and night shifts. And he would have to get home at a reasonable hour every day, help bathe the baby, feed him. Or her. Put him or her to bed. And look after Tamara as well. He knew that when it happened, this would be by far the biggest change in his life.

As he slid through the door and moved into the apartment, he said, "Hey, something smells great!"

Tamara popped out of the little kitchen area and launched herself into his arms. "It's your housewife doing some Cordon Bleu cooking."

"Housewife? More like apartment-wife," Mark said, brushing her lips with a quick kiss.

"That, too, shall pass," Tamara said. "Have a seat, supper is ready."

Mark sat and took a sip of water. "You know, I'm really worried about Dad."

Tamara rolled her eyes without attempting to show any empathy. "You've been worried about him non-stop for two years. Has anything that you've done even helped?"

"I don't know. Maybe not. But I'm a scientist. What's the control? If I hadn't been trying to help him get through this, maybe he'd be much worse. You know, major depression, unable to get out of bed–that kind of thing. And I do think that having Vi to look after has helped him. You see the way he looks at that dog, and the way she looks at him. Two lonely souls who need each other."

"I'll grant you that," Tamara said, "but what more can you do?"

"I don't know. Sign him up for an online dating service?"

"Mark!"

"Okay, I know, just kidding. But I really don't know any more." He attacked his spaghetti alla carbonara with relentless vigor. "When is Thanksgiving? Maybe we can cook up a small feast and that'll cheer him up."

Tamara frowned. "Mark, do you ever listen to me? We talked about this last week–I've got Thursday and Friday off, and you said we could drive out to see my parents. Danny's coming all the way from UCLA to Charlottesville, too."

"Oh. I guess I was a little preoccupied when you mentioned that."

"What do you mean 'mentioned it?'" Tamara shook her head. "You agreed! Do I have to get you to sign a contract every time we're scheduled to go visit my parents?"

Mark realized he was on shaky ground. "Okay, sorry. My fault. My memory isn't as good as it used to be, but I'm sure I agreed. I won't go back on my word." He smiled winningly. "How about if we invite your parents–and your brother Danny–out here to the wonderful DC area, and then we can include Dad?"

Twirling her pasta on her fork, Tamara tried to smile, but could feel her nerve ends grating. Mark was a good son–and probably had been a good brother–but he sure as hell didn't spend enough time looking after his own interests. Thinking back, she realized that he had always been like this, forever trying to be a good citizen and help those around him. She tried not to be bitter about this; after all, it was admirable. But the difference was that soon he would be a father, and even now, he should be looking out for his pregnant wife and the embryo growing inside her. He should be completing his applications, finding a permanent job with a better salary and benefits. Including life insurance. It was one thing to live as a young

17

couple, but the world turned on its head when a new baby was born. Was Mark ever going to grow up into a responsible head of a family? Or was he destined to forever be doing others' bidding? Sometimes she just wanted to knock some sense into him.

"Mark, how about those applications for faculty positions? Shouldn't you be spending more time getting those ready, instead of always worrying about your dad?"

"I told you, I really need to make my CV stronger–I need to get another paper or two in press, otherwise I might not be a strong enough candidate."

"I know, Mark–but you said that in the spring. It's fall now, and if you don't find something for the coming school year, what'll we do?" She shook her head in frustration. "This apartment is tiny, and once the baby is born, your productivity will go down." She looked at him sternly, but he averted his eyes. "You won't be able to just work 15 hour days–I'm going to need help. Besides, I don't know how we'll even afford day care on our current salaries."

Mark felt a pang in his chest. No, it was lower down, in his back. Damn stiff muscles, he thought. Too much tension. "Tamara, I can only do my best. I'm trying."

Tamara shook her head again. "Mark, sometimes I think you waste all of your energy worrying about others. Your dad. Your brother. It's about time for you to focus on yourself and your own family. Before it's too late."

Chapter Two

Eric smacked the screen on his desktop hard enough to shake it, but not hard enough to do any real damage. The computer was an instrument that he relied on, and he couldn't risk having to buy a new one. He looked at the numbers again, but they hadn't magically changed; he had lost over $6000 in day trading.

It just wasn't fair; no one cut him a break. Blacks–or what did they call themselves? African Americans? And the rest of those minorities–they were always complaining that they didn't get equal opportunities. But Eric knew that was all bull. It had nothing to do with race or skin color. There were those who were favored by their parents–and the rest of the world–and there were Erics, who always got shafted. The Erics of this world were always second-class, mistreated, and misjudged. They might be smarter, more gifted and talented, but they were held back by oppressive parents and family. This was the real injustice in the world, not the minority crap that they had everyone buying into.

Eric took a bite out of his taco; by now it was cold, and his beer had reached room temperature. Everything was conspiring against him. He climbed out of his office chair and headed for the toilet. Again. What the hell was going on? He had barely touched the beer, but was taking a leak every 15 minutes, or so it seemed. Nerves? But this time he saw something freaky... a spot of blood in the toilet bowl? Not wanting to see it, he flushed rapidly, washed his hands and went back to the computer. He should be looking for a job, but last time that had been a disaster. Some old fart telling *him* what to do, as if he were smarter than Eric. WTF?! They should have fired the old geek and given him a promotion, but he'd bet his father knew the owner and they planned the whole thing. Just to get back at him for embarrassing the family.

Being in prison had not been so bad, once Eric had gotten used to the idea. Steroids were easy to score, and he had bulked up in the gym. The food was bad, but it was almost worth it to tell that stuck-up lawyer that dad had sent him to piss off. The judge had asked him again and again, like some little brat, if he was sure he understood what it meant to decline legal representation. That lawyer wouldn't have done any better; he sold the drugs and that goddamn cop had videoed the whole thing. What was he going to say, "innocent"? Only some dickheaded mouthpiece would waste time on that angle.

Of course it was all his father's fault; if he had for once in his life actually helped him and lent him the money, Eric would never have needed to peddle drugs to pay back the loan sharks. What was 20 grand to the old man, anyway? So he wouldn't buy a new Prius every three years; he'd wait five instead. Would it really make any difference to him? Stingy old bastard. But maybe it wasn't so much the old man but his asshole brother. Eric would bet anything that the old man had asked him, and bro had said "Don't give it to him." Jealous bastard, he'd probably be thinking about his inheritance, even though 10 grand of that 20 was rightfully Eric's, in any case. Christ, he'd spent nearly two years in the slammer because of them.

He took another swig of the warm beer, burped out loud and cringed as something tugged and pulled at his lower back. What the hell? He hadn't even lifted yesterday at the gym. The throbbing increased, so Eric got up, headed for the bathroom again, urinated, and swallowed three more of those Tyelenol 3 pills—those ones with the codon, no, no, codeine, that was it. They did the trick, at least for a few hours. He sat back down in his chair, propped his feet upon the desk by the computer, lay his head back and dozed.

They stopped near the dam to admire the fall foliage; even Jeffrey couldn't deny the beauty of the pastel oranges, maple reds, and remaining greens. Ten years ago, he and Annie had made a trip out to New England in the fall to see the fall colors. They had enjoyed their visit to Massachusetts and the White Mountains of New Hampshire, but their joint conclusion later was that the fall in their home area was just as beautiful–if not more so. A Friday hike at the C & O Canal along the towpath, or walk down some segment of the Rock Creek Park had been something that he and Annie had done every year. And not just on Thanksgiving–nearly every weekend when time and weather permitted. But he was here with his son–well one of his sons–and his loyal dog. She was a pleasure, tail thumping, racing off leash through the crunching leaves, running back and forth to check up on Jeffrey, Mark and Tamara. She would never go more than twenty yards without racing back to the trio of humans; she probably did three miles for every mile that they walked.

Jeffrey was doing his best to act upbeat, and he knew what an effort his son and daughter-in-law were making to keep him connected, to ensure that he didn't slide into a rut from which there was no exit. He appreciated their effort, but it wasn't the quality of his own life that he was concerned about. He simply didn't want to disappoint Mark and Tamara. He couldn't bear failing anyone else in the family at this point. Two were more than enough.

"Water, Dad?" Mark asked passing him a bottle.

"What? Oh, yes, thanks," Jeffrey said, "It's actually warm out for this time of year. Let me get Vi's bowl out and give her a drink."

As Jeffrey removed his backpack to extract his dog's water dish, he was not oblivious to the glance that passed between Mark and Tamara, as if to say *See, that dog keeps him going.* But he didn't interrupt the silent communication. "It's really nice to have Vi around. She's great company."

Mark beamed. "I knew you'd love her." He bent down and succumbed to a series of facial licks. "She's so 'good-licking–' get it, Dad? Thanks, Girl. Now I need a towel."

Tamara said, "Mind if we have a short rest? There's a comfy-looking log over there by the side of the trail."

Jeffrey thought he noted another silent glance between the two of them, but he maintained his pretended ignorance. He even popped out a casual question. "How is it that your dad agreed to go to the mall with your mom and Danny? I thought he hated shopping as much as I do?"

Tamara laughed. "He does hate shopping! He took the Metro to *the* mall to take in some museums. Mom promised Danny to take him to Montgomery Mall–he needs a suit, and Dad doesn't have a clue."

"Or care," Mark interjected.

"Well, that's one of the sacrifices that parents–your mother, I mean–make for their kids," Jeffrey said, as he felt a pang of guilt well up again in his gut.

Jeffrey saw Mark wince, and knew that the subject was straying into dark waters. But in a second, Mark's creased furrow disappeared, and putting his arm around Tamara's shoulders, Mark said, "Dad, we have some good news to share with you!"

Jeffrey raised his eyebrows, knowing what was coming, but not wanting to spoil the surprise. "Tamara's pregnant. About six weeks! I'm going to be a father!"

Outwardly, Jeffrey smiled, but another pang of guilt hit him in the gut. What was wrong with him? Couldn't he be happy about soon being a grandfather? He was capable of pretending to share in others' happiness, but where were his *real* feelings? This was a little more complicated, though, and his smile wasn't like those frozen Botox ones where you could see how the person had their skin pulled tightly one way or another. He truly *wanted* to be happy for Mark and Tamara. But was he? Could he be? He just didn't know. In part, he wasn't sure that he knew exactly how happiness felt any more. Could it be that he had lost the capacity for real happiness when Annie died, just as someone who had lost his hearing or sight? After all, wasn't happiness ultimately relegated to bundles of nerves, synapses and chemical neurotransmitters? If one became sad, didn't those nerve connections weaken and atrophy, leaving one incapable of true happiness? He thought about this, and then thought some more. Wasn't it like libido in a person growing old? That desire was still there, the admiration of a beautiful woman–but without the ability to follow through? What would an eighty-year old be physically capable of, anyway?

"Earth to Dad! Are you there? What do you say?"

"Well," Jeffrey said, "I'd say this calls for a celebration."

Chapter Three

When his computer chimed to alert him of an incoming email, Jeffrey looked up from the computer screen and frowned. Ian Holmes, his colleague at Stanford, had sent him a note with *For your eyes only* as the heading. Jeffrey held his breath as he opened the email, a sensation burning in the pit of his stomach. He knew what this was about, and he also knew that he wasn't going to like it. Ian was a senior editor on the prestigious journal *Inside the Cell*, and Jeffrey guessed that this note had something to do with Jai's project and the Danfield lab.

In the meantime, he had managed to get through most of the editing of Jairaj's revised *Results* section, but of course there were several experiments missing–and those were not going to get done from the US Olympic gymnastics trials. Unlike his own work, which could essentially be done remotely from almost anywhere as long as he had his laptop and a wifi connection, a post-doc's success was mostly achieved through experiments in the lab. Sure, Jai could write up his results from home, or from wherever he was right now. But he wasn't going to be able to complete any of the remaining experiments from his hotel room. Although Jeffrey was reluctant to involve someone else in the project–mostly because it would probably take a few weeks until the new person was up to speed with the experimental system and by then Jai was scheduled to return–he felt that he could not sit by idly while the Danfield lab beat them to the punch. No, he would have to call in the cavalry.

Skimming through the note, Jeffrey felt his heart sink and his stomach turn sour: Ian had just received a manuscript from the Danfield lab for review, and being a close friend and colleague, he had written to alert Jeffrey that his competition was advancing.

Jeffrey knew that Ian was not acting strictly in a Kosher manner, as the submission of the manuscript should have been kept in confidence, and he was certain that Danfield would have listed him as a "conflict of interest" to ensure that he didn't receive the manuscript for review. It was obvious that Ian was giving him a courtesy call–he knew that Ian would be absolutely fair in his editorial treatment of the Danfield study–but he was giving Jeffrey a last minute reprieve to resubmit his own manuscript and try to publish before Danfield, rather than being left behind in the dust.

Jeffrey sat to write a short thank you note to his friend, and then pondered on the question of which post-doc would be best equipped to help out at short notice. He remembered that Jai said he'd speak to Reg. But that was not sufficient–Reg was busy with his own project. Jeffrey knew what he had to do; roll up his own sleeves and get to work in the lab. True, he had barely touched a pipette in the last seven years, but it was like riding a bicycle, after all. One doesn't forget how to ride a bicycle. He would just need to get some air into those tires first. Just as he prepared to launch himself from his chair, the phone rang. He picked up. "Jeffrey Coleman."

"Jeffrey, how are you doing?"

It was his institute director, Nigel Thorpe. Never having been involved in institute politics, which Jeffrey felt were best left to those who were not as interested as he was in the actual science, he did not know Dr. Nigel Thorpe very well. "Okay, thanks. How are you?"

"Very well, Jeffrey, in these tough times. Once Congress passes our budget, I'm hoping things will calm down, but you know, that's when I need to be on my guard, because the NIH director will be deciding how much to allocate to each of our institutes."

Jeffrey sighed. *Give me a scientific problem to tackle, but keep me from the headaches that Nigel endures every day.* It seemed as though every fall when the government fiscal year was scheduled to get started there was a threat of closing the government. Once this had happened, several years back, and despite the huge disruption to the country, Jeffrey's theory was that now that the barriers had been lowered, congressmen and women wouldn't hesitate to resort to such threats; if the president refused to back down on his promise to fund Planned Parenthood, there would be another imminent shutdown. Which meant that there would be no budget, and research at the NIH would grind to a halt. "I guess it's tough to be an optimist these days," he offered neutrally.

"It is, it is. But there's a group of us elite," he said, pronouncing it with a suspiciously southern intonation that sounded like *e-lite*, although Jeffrey knew that he was originally from New York City, "and we are the ones who know how to get things done, come hell or high water." The 'water' was still pronounced *wot-uh*; Nigel hadn't been able to reinvent himself into a total southerner, thought Jeffrey.

"Uh huh," Jeffrey said, not knowing how he was expected to reply. But he need not have worried about his response, as Nigel continued obliviously, "Well, Jeffrey, with Martin Jones' retirement there will be an opening for a branch chief and I'd like you to seriously consider the position."

Nearly dropping the phone, Jeffrey stammered, "Uh, pardon? Me? But I'm just a scientist."

"Ha ha. That's a good one, Jeffrey. I'll have to remember it when I give talks, meet the brass. 'Just a scientist.' That's great! We're all just scientists, Jeffrey. You and I and the NIH director. Only scientists can be branch chiefs and institute directors, don't you see?"

"Yes, no. I mean… " Jeffrey broke off momentarily trying to collect his thoughts. "What I mean is, I still have a lot to contribute to the scientific enterprise, and that I'm not exactly, well, equipped to focus on administrative issues."

"Jeffrey, no need to be humble. I know your capabilities. I reviewed your tenure, way back, and your promotions. You don't have to slow down your research program." Nigel paused, and Jeffrey could imagine a fatherly pat on his head had they been meeting in person. "In fact," Nigel went on, his voice lowered to a whisper, "this would actually advance your own program, because you could increase your own budget and the size of your group. That's one of the advantages of being in a leadership role."

Jeffrey considered this. It was true that most branch chiefs had large research groups. And he knew that there was a pretty significant jump in salary. "But what about all the administrative duties? Won't I be sitting from morning to night in windowless rooms, writing reports and pushing paper?"

Nigel seemed ready for this. "I won't lie to you, Jeffrey. Of course this comes with administrative duties. Leadership requires decisions, and that's what you'll need to do. But most of these are important decisions that will impact the research in your lab and in the rest of the branch. Hiring new faculty, allocating budgets to the other principal investigators in your branch. If you are not involved in making those decisions, I'll have to choose someone else to make them. Someone less capable and fair than you. Do you really want to force me to do that?"

Jeffrey stared at the ceiling, feeling a migraine coming on. "When do you need my decision?"

He could hear the lighter tone in Nigel's voice, "Just take your time, Jeffrey. I know you'll do what's right."

Eric pumped his fists in the air—the Dow was up, and things were turning around. He knew it was best not to sell those stocks, that they had hit rock bottom and couldn't go any lower. Let those suckers panic and sell out. He would wait out the market and the rebound would be his—all his. He reclined back in his chair, his elbow on the armrest and his chin nestled on his knuckle. For the millionth time he thought, *Should I call Dad?*

He knew that his father would never abandon him, but he also knew that Jeffrey would never again make the first move and reach out to Eric. Dad had given up after the trial, when Eric had refused the stupid lawyer. But in his gut—which didn't feel right, and had him constantly trotting back and forth to the toilet—he wanted to show his father that he was a success. That he was just as smart as everyone else in the family. He could call him and tell him about the opportunity to get in now, while the stocks were cheap and rack up a bundle. So what if Dad hadn't lent him the money when he really needed it; he didn't need to be petty. Eric smiled patronizingly; he would show Dad that he was above all that. That he, Eric, could forgive him.

Just then his cell phone rang. "Yeah?" There was no immediate reply, and Eric—coupled with the pain in his lower back side—felt irritation that he could no longer suppress. "Who the hell is this and what do you want?"

The voice on the other end of the line was grainy—not exactly warped by a muffler of some sort, but definitely not easy to characterize. "This is your last chance. Either fork over the dope you stole, or suffer the consequences."

Eric knew that this had to be the Valencia brothers. He had hoped that they would leave him alone after he got out of jail, but those guys had the memories of elephants. And if he wasn't careful, they'd squash him like an elephant stepping on a banana.

As the pain reached his belly, making him want to run to the toilet, he answered hurriedly, "I told you guys that I don't have the stuff. I didn't take it. Someone must've hacked into my email and found the hiding place. I swear."

The voice, likely one of the Valencia lieutenants, chuckled and then abruptly stopped. "Listen up. This is a courtesy call. That means that we're trying to be nice. The stuff was in your hands, and it belongs to us. We don't give a shit if you smoked it, baked it, ate it, sat on it or fucking farted on it, but we expect the stuff or you gotta pay for it. $15,000 plus, let's see, a bit of interest over the few years you weren't around, that would make $23,000. Even."

Eric was sweating, and feeling as though he was going to toss his cookies. Or tacos. "Are you guys nuts? Twenty three grand? How am I supposed to come up with that much dough?"

"That's your problem. But from experience, I can tell you that it's remarkable how creative guys like you can get when your life is on the line. I'm sure you'll find a way."

Coming out of the toilet, Eric barely reached the hallway when his phone rang again.

"What?! What the fuck do you guys want now?"

"Coleman, this is Pit. Relax, man–don't get your undies in a twist. Gotta job for you."

"Jesus, Pit. Godammit, you scared the bejesus out of me."

"Listen mate, I got something for you."

Eric sighed. "I served my time, I'm done with that. No more drugs."

"Coleman, I'm telling you, I got some easy cash to make, listen up."

"I'm listening. Long as it isn't drugs or armed robbery."

"Well, listen good. My buddy Tink got in on this, and it's a piece of cake. Turns out that a lot of rich people from Potomac– you know, these guys with four car garages and such–like to leave their cars at Reagan National when they go out of town."

"So? I'm not into car theft. Once you boost a car, it's tough to unload it. Anyway, that's grand felony."

He could hear Pit spitting or clearing his throat. "Nah, it's not car boosting," Pit said, a tinge of scorn in his voice, followed by another unappetizing sound from his throat. "Seriously man, I'm not that stupid. This is much better."

"Well?"

"Turns out that many of these rich-asses leave their garage openers in the car, and fly off around the world."

"And? You plan on driving around the greater DC area with your finger on the opener waiting for a garage to pop open?"

"For a smart guy, you can be a pretty dumb ass. These richies also tend to leave their driver's registration sittin' in the glove compartment. How about that? With their address in black and white!"

Eric thought about that momentarily. "Brilliant, Pit, but I can't get involved in B & E. I don't want to go back inside if we get caught."

"Listen man, I cut you a break. Tink'll pop the cars, and me and him'll go in—you know, clean house." He cackled with pleasure and made another unseemly sound. "All you gotta do is drive us, stay in the car and keep watch. You know, stay with us on the phone 'til we get out. Tink says he give you 20%."

Feeling pain again in his lower back area, on the right side, Eric wriggled uncomfortably in his chair. He wouldn't make 23 grand, but it could be a promising start. "Let me think about it. I got some medical issues to look after. When do you need an answer?"

"Yesterday," Pit said. "But you got 'til the end of the day. If I don't get no word from you, we offer this to someone else."

Chapter Four

"Branch chief? Dad that's great!"

Jeffrey felt a wave of relief wash over him at the heartfelt happiness that Mark was showing at his new promotion—although truthfully he wasn't sure whether it was a promotion or demotion. "It's not something I ever aspired to, or really seriously considered," Jeffrey said into the phone. "But Nigel Thorpe can be pretty persuasive."

"Dad, stop apologizing for taking the position. You deserve it!"

"Thanks, Mark. I'm just not sure how cut out I am for the administrative side of it." Jeffrey continued his circuits around his little apartment, with Vi following him closer than his shadow.

"I'm sure you'll be a great decision maker; efficient and anti-bureaucratic."

Jeffrey grunted. "You know, Mark, right now I'm worried about taking on anything that'll interfere with my ability to do science. Remember I told you about the competition that we have from the Danfield lab? With Jai's project?" He didn't wait for a reply. "Well, you know how it is—apparently they submitted a manuscript, and if they scoop us, we'll be left mopping up the crumbs."

Mark knew what that was like. Early in his own postdoctoral studies he had made some remarkably interesting findings on how neurons transmit signals under conditions of stress. His mentor had wanted to "go for gold"—shoot for the most prestigious journal, as he had recognized the potential impact of Mark's findings. The trade off, Mark soon learned, was that it took a lot longer, and in the meantime, there were other groups also searching for the Holy Grail. It was a little like playing Hearts: one could be conservative, and strive to keep a low profile and collect as few hearts as possible.

But then there was the other strategy–getting control. "Shooting the moon" as it was called, where a player would attempt to collect all thirteen hearts and the Queen of Spades. A successful bid would give the happy player zero points in that round, while all other players incurred 26 negative points. But–and here was the catch–if the player missed even a single heart, he could end up with 25 negative points.

"I hear you, Dad. But I know you well enough to realize that you can handle it."

Unable to deal with Mark's positive attitude, Jeffrey changed the subject. "Tell me, Mark, how's Tamara doing? Is she still feeling the nausea, or has it settled down?

"Much better this week. She has another appointment Friday, and I think they'll be doing an ultrasound. We're really excited."

"I am too," Jeffrey said.

Tamara put her palm gently on Mark's forehead. "You don't feel warm," she said. "But I'm used to dealing with children, so I'm not sure."

"I took some acetaminophen a couple hours ago, but these past couple of days I've been really uncomfortable." He looked at her worriedly. "You're a nurse, do you think I should call Dr. Smith?"

Tamara knew that Mark was not often sick, so if he was complaining, he would probably be best to have it checked out. But she also didn't want to frighten him. "Well, my philosophy is 'what do you have to lose?' We have medical coverage, so you may as well get it looked at. It's probably nothing serious, but why stress out?"

Mark nodded thoughtfully. "I guess you're right. I didn't want to have to take time off work, but what's a couple hours if it'll clear my mind?"

"Tamara, how are you?" Jeffrey asked. Not wanting to meddle, he hesitated slightly and then, unable to contain himself, "Is everything okay with the baby?"

There was a long pause on the phone. "The baby? Oh, sure. Yeah. We had an ultrasound this week–everything's right on schedule. And," she breathed out deeply, "it's not twins."

Jeffrey laughed. "I'll bet that's a relief. I can tell you—as I'm sure Mark can—twins can be a handful, and not just the early years."

"Oh, I know. I mean, I've seen it. I was concerned that Mark might genetically predispose us to having twins."

"I think it's more likely to come from the mother's side, but I hear you."

Again, there was an awkward pause on the phone. From experience, Mark was usually the one to contact his dad—not that Jeffrey didn't get along with Tamara. He liked his daughter-in-law and had a deep respect for her simple tastes and down-to-earth personality. But she wasn't one to just pick up the phone and chat with him. Yes, it was decidedly out of character.

Not wanting to ask if everything was okay again, Jeffrey said, "So was Mark as relieved as you?"

This tack had the required effect, because Tamara answered immediately. "Well, uh, relieved isn't exactly in his vocabulary right now. He's having a rough time."

"You mean getting used to the pregnancy and upcoming life changes? Or at work?"

Tamara was silent for what seemed like an eternity. And then Jeffrey could hear muffled sobs. This was no time to show respect for her privacy. "Tamara, what is it?"

Now she was crying—bawling loudly—into the phone. "He hasn't been feeling so well these past few weeks, and they did some blood tests, and finally an MRI yesterday, and—"

She broke off again, and Jeffrey, with a queasy feeling working its way through his innards, gripped his cell phone so hard that his knuckles were turning white, prodded again gently. "What? What is it?"

"He's got this kidney problem," she said in between sobs. "Polycystic Kidney Disease. They call it PKD."

Jeffrey felt as though a brick had fallen on his head. He sat down, struggling to maintain his composure. The last thing he needed was to make Tamara feel worse. "Well, I should talk to him and see exactly what this is about. I have a friend here, Ravi, who's a nephrologist."

Tamara sniffled again. "And to think that I see really sick kids every day at work—it just seems so different when it happens to someone close."

31

Ain't that the truth, thought Jeffrey. But he said, "Can I talk to him? Or is he resting?"

"He finally just dozed off," Tamara said, "But—would you be willing to go with him to the nephrologist on Monday? I think—I think he'd appreciate that."

"Of course," Jeffrey said. "What are fathers for?"

As he lay in bed on his stomach, despite the feeling that someone was standing on his back trying to drill a hole just under his rib cage, Eric was satisfied. He knew that he was a cut above those two hoodlum-losers, and after all he had only driven the car for them. He hadn't really broken any law; they were the ones who did the stealing, and they would have done it with or without his driving. So why not take advantage of the situation? He had even done some good; he had seen that the brick house on the corner was owned by an older couple, and had steered those losers—Pit and that moron Tink—away. Told them that he saw a big German shepherd in the yard. It was a *mitzvah*, as his old man might have said, keeping them from stealing from pensioners—if he hadn't been the driver, these old people might be out on the streets. Besides, the rest of these wealthy victims were probably all insured to the hilt. Why, Eric would bet that they came out making money out of these thefts. Probably claimed more was stolen than Pit and Tink actually took. And who cared how much those goddamn insurance companies were losing. Those A-holes were ripping off everyone in the country, including him. What the hell! A night driving on the town, not even doing anything really against the law, and he had another ten grand to invest.

Maybe he would call Dad. The old man himself wasn't so bad; it was that peckerwood of a brother that really turned Dad against him. He could even ask him if he knew a quack that might have some idea about that pain. Could prescribe some good meds—legally, not just these knock-off narcotics that you get on the street and that wore off in an hour. Some real stuff that would keep him comfortable without making him woozy.

Eric thought about Mark and his stomach recoiled, and he needed the toilet again, damn, something in his plumbing wasn't right! Mark had always been against him, from day one. Perhaps even before day one. Eric imagined Mark pushing him around in the womb, the two of them vying for the best position. And he thought of Mom, who never judged him like Dad did. She was always there for him, until she wasn't anymore. She would have visited him in the slammer; damn well wouldn't have come with her forefinger wagging in the air with that *I told you so* look. No, she would've talked to him about how he was doing, asked if he needed anything. It was enough that the goddamn jury had put him away—he didn't need his own father to add to the verdict. Christ, what a bunch of hypocrites. Except Mom. And she was gone.

Eric remembered the day in 7th grade that they had come home with their first middle school report cards. Mark had ridiculed him on the bus ride home; he had said with that disdainful know-it-all look, "Only a 3.0 in algebra? Didn't know you were having a hard time. I could help you."

He knew that Mark didn't really want to help him; it was all about making him look bad in front of Dad. Eric wasn't about to accept help anyway, but he was sure that if he had, Mark would be yakking about it day and night, making sure that their parents saw what a great brother he was. And of course, that he was smarter than Eric. No, there had been only one thing to do, and even today he felt not a whit of guilt. He had smiled at Mark, and said, "Thanks, but I don't need your stupid help," and proceeded to tear Mark's report card in half and then in half again. Mark had made a grab for it, but Eric had always been stronger, and unafraid to use elbows and knees. And he promptly tossed the pieces out the bus window while Mark screamed and screamed. And Godammit, it was worth it, to see the tears streaming down Mark's sulky face. Dad had grounded him and had taken only Mark to the Orioles games, but it had been *so* worth it. Since that time he had been grounded so often he felt like an electric outlet. But even today he could still see Mark's bloated face, tears streaming down his cheeks. What a baby!

But the very worst had been that stupid Bar Mitzvah. He knew that even Mark didn't care about reading from the Torah—no, it was all about showing that he could do it better than Eric. And when Eric had gotten up to the pulpit after Mark and stumbled through his reading, he had sensed a huge sigh of relief emanating from his father—that Eric had finished and that there were no more embarrassments yet to come. Little did he know, thought Eric, that

33

for the rest of his life one of his sons would be a major embarrassment to his family.

Eric reached for his phone and picked it up, intent on finally calling his father. The pain had become excruciating. But before he could tap out the number–his dad wasn't exactly on speed dial–the pain became so great that it numbed his brain and paralyzed his fingers. Something was seriously wrong, and there was no time to lose. He barely punched out the 9-1-1 before collapsing.

Chapter Five

When Mark came out of the examination room, Jeffrey patted his shoulder and said, "Sit." And as Mark took a seat next to a table covered with *House and Garden*, *People*, and other peacefully-inane magazines, Jeffrey asked, "So what's next? Will Dr. Ramsey call us in to talk?"

Mark shrugged. "I think so. He may have to go over all the tests first, but the nurse said that he'd call me." He looked pleadingly at his father. "Dad, I'm really scared."

Jeffrey forced himself not to look away. "Let's take this one step at a time. We can't get ahead of ourselves. Let's see what the doctor has to say, what he recommends. Then we'll set in place the best plan that we can."

Mark nodded, and they sat silently for a few minutes until the nurse came out and asked Mark to come back to Dr. Ramsey's office. "Is it okay if my dad comes?" Mark asked.

She smiled and nodded and they followed her in. Dr. Ramsey was a tall, thin, reedy bald man in a white lab coat who looked to be in his early sixties. He got up from behind his desk, on which sat a laptop with an enormous screen, and shook hands with both Mark and Jeffrey. After exchanging a few pleasantries and finding out that both his patient and his father were scientists, Ramsey got down to business.

"Mark, as we discussed last week, we can confirm your diagnosis of autosomal dominant polycystic kidney disease, or for short, PKD. The tests that we have done leave no doubt."

Despite already knowing this, Mark looked crestfallen. "But Dr. Ramsey, if this is an autosomal dominant disease, then how is it that only now–at age 29–am I being diagnosed? That doesn't make sense to me. Are you sure?"

Dr. Ramsey nodded. "There is still a lot we don't understand about PKD. And one of the main issues is how an autosomal dominant disease doesn't become apparent at birth. Or even prenatally." He released air slowly through his mouth. "Generally, there are two hypotheses: one is that while the defective gene is clearly inherited in a dominant manner–directly from parent to child–there may need to be two hits for gene inactivation."

Jeffrey cut in. "If I understand correctly, Dr. Ramsey, then either my deceased wife or I are not just 'carriers' but one of us has the defective gene–but that something, say, in the environment set off Mark's inherited defective gene, but not mine or my wife Annie's?"

Dr. Ramsey nodded slowly. "You've got the idea. Unlike recessive diseases, where two carriers produce a child with both alleles defective and cause disease, here we know that one parent with a deficient gene is enough to transmit the disease. Sometimes the parent is sick, and not the child, and other times it's the child and not the parent, as in this case. And sometimes, we assume, both parent and child might have the defective gene, but since no one is sick, we never actually know."

"What's the other possibility?" Mark asked. "You said there were two hypotheses."

"Yes, Mark," Dr. Ramsey said. "They aren't mutually exclusive–meaning both possibilities might be correct. As we discussed last week, all these symptoms you've been having–the kidney pain in your lower back, the blood in the urine, and even the high blood pressure–these all probably result from the large cysts that have developed in your kidneys."

Jeffrey said, "Yeah, I read that one of two proteins, called PKD1 and PKD2 are probably responsible."

"That's right," Dr. Ramsey said. "The thing is, the formation of these large cysts may take many years. That's why we think the onset occurs at such a relatively late age, and not early in childhood."

Mark was tapping his foot impatiently. "Okay, fine. So we know more or less what causes this, and why it's taken so long for me to feel any symptoms. But that's not the point. I want to know what the treatment is, and how my prognosis will be. I didn't see much on Wikipedia about that, and I have a baby coming in seven months." He suddenly paled, looking stricken. "Wait… what about my baby? Will he… will she… will the baby inherit this? Oh, what a cluster-fuck!"

Neither Dr. Ramsey nor Jeffrey reacted to the odd sound of cursing from Mark, who sat rocking back and forth, unable to focus. Jeffrey put his arm around Mark's shoulders again, and quietly said, "Let's just take this one step at a time, okay. Let's hear out Dr. Ramsey."

Mark made the tiniest of nods with his head, and Dr. Ramsey took that for a signal to continue with the agenda of the meeting. "Unfortunately, Mark, this is one disease that medical science has yet to find a treatment."

"You mean it's fatal, and I'm going to die," Mark interjected bitterly, squirming in his chair.

Jeffrey said, "Come on, Mark, let Dr. Ramsey finish."

"Well," Dr. Ramsey said, "While there is no 'cure,' I think we need to get you tissue-typed and try for a kidney transplant."

"And that'll solve the problem?"

Dr. Ramsey shifted forward in his chair, and leaned over placing his elbows on the desk and his chin in his hands. "Mark, I don't want to get your hopes up, because a transplant is no small thing. But, yes, if we were able to perform a successful transplant with a properly matched kidney–and assuming you took the transplant well, you would have a good chance of living a long life. Sure, you'd be on immunosuppressants–medication to prevent your immune system from attacking and rejecting the new kidney. And you might be more susceptible to infections. But those are generally workable issues."

A flicker of hope enveloped Mark's stricken features. "Really?"

"Yes," said Dr. Ramsey. "I have patients in their seventies today, and they're going strong. While there are of course no guarantees–you know, I could be crossing the street and get hit by a bus. Or a meteorite–with a bit of luck, you'll be okay."

Mark now looked determined. "Okay. Let's plan on that."

Jeffrey rolled over and glanced at the LED display beside his bed: 3:14 am. Before he even had a chance to groan and seek refuge under his pillow, he could feel the warm breath of Vi and her hot tongue licking his cheek. Reeling from the onslaught, he sat up, propped a couple pillows behind his back and neck, and flipped on the lamp on the night table.

The initial tissue typing for Mark and Jeffrey at the Georgetown Transplant Institute in DC had been done, and preliminary results were not expected for about two weeks. Until then, Jeffrey knew that it would be impossible to get a good night's sleep. The doctor had been cautiously optimistic that Jeffrey would be a reasonable match. Although it was not explicitly stated, they all knew that having only a single living parent significantly decreased the statistical possibility of Mark getting a matched kidney within the time frame needed. About 30% of kidneys transplanted came from close family relatives.

Wearily scratching Vi behind the ears and listening to her satisfied sighs, he reflected for the hundredth time on the horrible similarities between the situation now with Mark and what he and Annie had gone through. He hadn't been able to sleep through most of it then, either. Annie had–at least some of the time. He had pretended to sleep, as if things were normal. It had been critical that she maintained a routine to keep up her spirits and strength. Ultimately that hadn't helped. Well, perhaps it had, because Annie had remained calm as a rock throughout. But no, that was how Annie was–she always had that practical, optimistic make-the-best-out-of-the-situation outlook. Like a goddamn boy scout. Well, technically, a girl scout. Whatever–he was too tired for these conversations with himself. He slid out of the bed, gobbled a Xanax down without even the benefit of any water, and slid back under the sheets.

Tamara loaded the strong Columbian coffee into the machine and flipped the switch, waiting impatiently for the gurgling to begin. It was one of those days where she had the afternoon shift, and Mark had already gone to work–he had promised to continue preparing his applications for faculty positions and to try to keep his mind away from pessimistic scenarios until they knew where he stood with the transplant. She had told him they'd take it one day at a time–by breaking time down into manageable units, it was possible, for the most part, to stay sane, and believe that the next time segment would be better–but she had a feeling it was going to feel more like one hour at a time, or even one minute. Of course when lightning struck so close to home, living this philosophy was no easy matter. But she shook her head as she poured a cup of coffee–it was no easy matter on the oncology floor either.

Tamara loved Mark, for all his faults. The dental floss that occasionally missed the bathroom trash can, the bits of stubble that he routinely forgot to wash down the drain, his irritating habit of nodding his head when she told him a long story, and then to look up and say "What? Sorry, I was thinking of an experiment in the lab." She always forgave him because he was, after all, a good person. He loved her, respected her, and he was so different from the many macho-guys she had dated years ago. He stood up for gender equality, and she fully believed him when he said that he would be as happy or even happier if their baby was a girl. From her friends at work, she knew that this was a rare trait; even the most equal opportunity men seemed to have these dreams of playing baseball or basketball with their sons. She was certain in this respect that Mark was exceptional.

Tamara was also distinctly aware of Mark's weaknesses. He could be moody, although she had never seen him depressed. But then again, he really never had cause to be depressed–at least until now. And although he had always been in good shape physically–or so they had both thought–he'd always been a complainer. His shoulder was sore, his feet hurt from standing too long, his back ached from sitting at the microscope for hours and hours. She did not think he would have lasted long as a construction worker. Or a registered nurse.

She recalled her first date with him, back when he had been a graduate student and she had been in nursing school. She hadn't been able to find a free table in the medical center cafeteria, so she asked Mark if he minded if she sat at his table. Mark smiled, saying, "My pleasure." By the end of their lunch, in his geeky but winning manner, he asked her if she would accompany him to judge a high school science fair the next Saturday.

"A high school science fair? Seriously?"

"Sure, it's fun. Then we can go for dinner when the judging ends. You can help me–as a nursing student you know a lot of science."

Oddly enough, it *had* been fun, and Mark was clearly in his element, talking with kids about how well their plants grew under different conditions of light and nutrients, and what important controls they had done—or should have done. They really hit it off with each other, too, finding a range of common interests. In fact, after that afternoon, they had never really been apart from each other for much more than a day of work.

It was a cool, cloudy day as Jeffrey, Mark and Tamara slowly climbed out of the Prius in the parking lot at Georgetown Hospital and headed for the kidney unit where the tissue typing was done. Dr. Ramsey had promised to join them in their meeting with Dr. Jergen, the head of the tissue typing division. Jeffrey saw the bags under Mark's eyes, and he knew Mark was probably noting his own haggard appearance. He saw at once that Tamara was the strong one; she had to be, taking care of kids with cancer every day. He marveled at how she was able to hold it together, day in and day out. Dealing with kids who had infusions, catheters, chemotherapy, and hair falling out. How could one stay sane and not start throwing pots and pans at the sky, trying to knock God out of His apathy?

Mark, on the other hand, did not have that toughness about him. He had always been good and well-meaning, but hadn't stood up well to teasing and bullying. He had never been able to shrug off those abusive attacks as so many other kids his age had learned to do. It wasn't that he had accepted it and refused to fight, but rather that he was confused by it.

As the automatic glass door swung open and Mark and Tamara entered just ahead of him, Jeffrey caught snatches of Tamara's pragmatism, "Don't assume the worst," and "Let's wait for the doctor's interpretation before jumping to conclusions." Being a parent was never easy, and sure hadn't gotten easier over time, Jeffrey thought, and followed them inside.

A large, moon-faced man with European-styled dark, rectangular-framed glasses, Dr. Jergen invited them to sit down at the round table in his spacious office. The walls, Jeffrey noted, were tastefully decorated with framed prints of impressionist paintings— most likely purchased downtown at the National Gallery of Art. The office obviously served as a consultation room, and the Monet and Manet posters lent a homey feel, an allusion to all the beauty in the world.

As Jeffrey quickly realized, however, Dr. Jergen was not a man who avoided getting to the point by pushing small talk. Once they had been seated, he turned to Mark and immediately said, "We have the results from your tissue typing," and nodding at Jeffrey, "and from the potential match with Dr. Coleman's HLA."

"Please call me Jeffrey."

Dr. Jergen smiled. "Well, it'll make it easier saying Mark and Jeffrey, rather than confusing two Dr. Colemans." He continued. "You both are familiar with HLA matching?"

When father and son nodded silently, Dr. Jergen said, "Well, just to make sure we're on the same page, the Human Leukocyte Antigens, or HLA markers as we call them, are a measure of how close the two of you are with respect to recognition by the immune system." He took off his glasses and polished an imaginary speck of dust. "If your HLA markers were identical, we would have little concern that with you as a donor, and Mark's kidney transplant wouldn't have much chance of being rejected—which of course would be great."

Mark cut in. "The way you say that sounds as though Dad's kidney won't be a match?"

"Slow down, Mark. That's not what I said. That was a hypothetical. In truth, most family members have parts of their HLA that are closely aligned and others that are less so. That is the case here." He drew a little schematic diagram with a marker on a dry-erase board. "Jeffrey is a potential match for you—but quite honestly, very far from perfect. If we had to proceed today with an urgent transplant, we would definitely give it a shot. I'd say it's an 80% chance of success. If you were in worse condition," he smiled at Mark, "we wouldn't even hesitate." Now he turned to Jeffrey. "But since you are a living donor, as we call it, let's give it a little time and see if any kidney pops up." He looked back and forth at the two Colemans. "The good thing is that we always have your kidney in reserve for Mark, whenever necessary."

Jeffrey shook his head. "Isn't 80% as good as it gets? Why wouldn't we just do the transplant now?"

Dr. Ramsay chimed in. "Actually, there's a possibility of a random donor popping up with a better likelihood for success."

Mark looked stricken. "You mean while I suffer, we wait for someone who would be a better match to die?"

The two older men glanced at each other, and Dr. Jergen answered, "Well, Mark, since you aren't in imminent danger—at least right now—this is the cautious way to proceed. It's possible that your condition might deteriorate in the near future—I won't lie to you—but it's also possible that you'll remain relatively stable over the next six to twelve months, and during that time a better matched donor might turn up."

Tamara, who had been silent until now, said, "But isn't there some danger in waiting? I mean, like the damage to the kidneys affecting other systems such as the heart, bladder and so on? Wouldn't you do the transplant right away if you had a better match?"

Dr. Jergen nodded. "There's always that risk, and if we had a 90% match, we would schedule the transplant right away." He shrugged. "But we can only work with what we have—I mean, if we had a perfect match, that would be optimal. But we don't."

Tamara fiercely ignored the pleading look in Jeffrey's eyes. "But we do. I mean, we do have a perfect match, and we don't even have to do HLA typing to be sure."

Tamara and the two Dr. Colemans sat at Saxby's coffee shop just a few blocks southeast of the medical center. They all had lattes and pastries, but the two men had ignored their food. Tamara noticed that Jeffrey seemed anxious to avoid looking at her, while Mark glared at both of them. She couldn't take the silence any longer and finally broke out. "So I said his name. What, are you both playing martyr here?" She glared back at Mark. "You're going to be a father in a few months time! Don't you think it's irresponsible not to even follow up on it? I mean, a perfectly matched twin brother—how many people needing kidney transplants have such an opportunity?"

Jeffrey shifted in his chair, crossing one leg over the other, and then reversing his position. "Tamara." It came out as a whisper. "I don't think you underst—"

"The hell I don't!" She turned toward him. "What kind of chickenshit parent are you? Send one son to the gallows rather than even talk to your other son?"

He looked away, and she pounced on Mark. "Well? Which of you are going to contact him? Or I am going to have to do it?"

Mark gritted his teeth. "He'd never agree. He'd probably be happy to hear I'm so ill. I won't give him the satisfaction."

Jeffrey turned toward him. "Mark. Listen. Tamara may be right–"

"Of course I'm right," Tamara snorted. "I'm–"

Jeffrey held up his hand, requesting that she let him continue. "I know that I swore I wouldn't ever speak to him again after the way he treated us and the lawyer, not without an apology. But things are different now–Tamara's right. This is life and death."

"Ah geez, Dad. He's just going to spit in my face. Forget it! I don't want any favors from him. I'll wait for a matched donor, or manage with your kidney. Uh, thanks by the way."

Tamara pointed her finger at Mark, coming dangerously close to his eyes. "Shut up, Mr. Macho! Enough of this crap about your brother! Don't you start pretending that you can wait this out– there's a baby on the way, and I don't want him–or her–growing up without a father because you two are too proud to ask for help."

"No, Tamara," Jeffrey said, "I will call him. If I can find him."

"What's the point? He's not going to give me a kidney." Mark rolled his eyes in frustration. "Tamara, you've never even met him, but he's a mean son of a..."

"We have to pursue every possible avenue. For the baby's sake and for my sake. You told me that you haven't been in contact with him for over ten years. How do you know he hasn't changed?"

Mark didn't seem frightened anymore–just angry. "What, changed in jail? Did he bother calling Dad when he got out? With me it's a total loss, but with Dad? All he's ever wanted from him is money–to pay for drugs, loan sharks, whatever. Do you think he gives a shit about anyone in the family?"

"Then I'll talk to him," Tamara said. "If neither of you is willing to even try, then I will. I'll just call, introduce myself and invite him to go out for coffee. To hell with your male pride."

"He'll never go," Mark said.

"Mark, just be quiet for a minute," Jeffrey said, and turning back to Tamara. "Tamara, easy does it. I understand your feelings, believe me. But I'll call him. As uncomfortable as the situation is, I'm his father, and I need to try."

Mark was losing his patience. "Yeah, Dad. He'll hit you up for another loan for drug money. Brilliant."

Jeffrey showed just the hint of a smile. "That might not be so bad after all. If he needs money badly enough, perhaps I can come to some kind of an arrangement with him."

Chapter Six

Jeffrey nodded. "Yes."

"What do you mean, yes?" Jai asked, confused. "If we think that the kinase pathway is involved, then we need to re-examine the whole system!"

Jeffrey opened his eyes wider and looked at the film containing Jai's results again. "You're right, I'm sorry–I wasn't focused for a minute–it's… never mind. No, we don't need to examine the system again. These data support our contentions. How many times have you repeated this?"

Jai breathed out slowly, the tension exiting his muscles as he realized that Jeffrey was back in command. "This is the fourth repeat. Experiments one, three, and four all gave very similar results. I had a technical issue on the second experiment and we couldn't assess the results."

"Let's start writing up the data and get this revision ready for resubmission. But to be safe, how about one more repeat in parallel with the writing?"

"Exactly what I planned," Jai said. "I'll have it by the end of the weekend."

As Jai was scooping up his data, Jeffrey's phone rang.

"Hello?"

"Is this Jeffrey Coleman?" said a deep bass voice that sounded unfamiliar to Jeffrey.

"Yes. Who is this?"

"I'm Rob Danfield–from UCSF."

"Ah," said Jeffrey, at a loss for words. He noticed that Jai was about to leave, so he motioned to him to sit down and said, for Jai's benefit, "What can I do for you, Dr. Danfield?"

The voice on the other end of the line laughed ominously. "Just call me Rob."

"Okay, Rob. I'm familiar with your work—it's odd that we never ran into each other at meetings. So how can I be of service?" He rolled his eyes at Jai, figuring that this was some kind of trick.

"Actually," said Rob Danfield, "We did run into each other at the BCB meeting in Prague. You may not remember, but I gave a keynote talk there—and I attended the 'breaking news session' where you gave a ten minute talk—I even asked you a question afterward."

Jeffrey, who didn't recall any of that, recognized a put-down when he heard one. Danfield was essentially telling him that while he had only been asked to deliver a measly ten-minute talk, he, Danfield, had been the center of attention and had been honored with a full one-hour talk. It didn't matter that Jeffrey wasn't really in the field, and had gone to learn about a new area of research—and to get away from DC and try and recover from his wife's death. Danfield was showing him who was the more highly-respected scientist—or so he thought. But what did he want from Jeffrey?

Jeffrey watched as Jai now rolled his eyes at the pettiness of Danfield broadcast over the speaker-phone. "Well Rob, now that you mention it, I do remember that meeting. Unfortunately, I missed your talk, though." He didn't bother adding that he had elected to wander the streets of the city instead—no need to respond to pettiness with more pettiness.

"I'm calling," said Danfield, "because I know that we are both working on a very similar angle, and I thought that neither of us would really want to scoop the other. You know, it wouldn't be good for either of us."

"Indeed," said Jeffrey.

"I was thinking that we should probably have an open dialog running. You know, keep each other informed as to our status, and communicate with each other before submitting manuscripts."

Jeffrey frowned, and nodded to Jai. "That sounds like a very generous plan. Very fair—probably excellent for our post-docs."

"So what's the status of your study—is it ready for submission to a journal? You must be way ahead of us, because we have a long time to go until we'll be ready to submit."

Jeffrey continued to frown, shaking his head in astonishment in Jai's direction, and at the same time shrugging with his palms face up. What the hell was Danfield playing at? He wanted to know whether Jeffrey had resubmitted his manuscript, when he knew full well that he would receive the resubmission for review? And in the meantime he wanted a promise that Jeffrey would inform him when they were ready to submit, while he, Danfield, had *already* submitted his own manuscript? And yet he was lying... saying that he still had a long way to go until submission? This guy had some balls! "No," he said, "I haven't. So you haven't submitted your study yet?"

Danfield was silent for a moment. But only for a moment. "No, not yet. We're still trying to work out the pathway, and only once we have that will we be ready."

Jeffrey was able to grunt an "Uh huh." In the meantime, he scribbled madly on his scrap paper and passed it to Jai: *He's lying through his teeth.*

As soon as Jai left the office, Jeffrey called Mark. "How are you feeling?"

"A little better, Dad, thanks. So... have you been able to reach him?"

"He's not at the apartment he moved into when he got out of—well when he got out. I asked his landlord if she'd gotten a forwarding address, but she said no. So I don't know... "

Jeffrey heard Mark report the update to Tamara, and then he heard her say, "We need to hire a private investigator. They have all kinds of websites that can find people through driver's registration and so on. Unless he's really gone nuts and stolen someone's identity, I bet even an amateur PI could find him."

"Is it worth the money and effort?" Mark asked.

Jeffrey heard Tamara's prompt response: "Is it *worth* it? With you potentially going on dialysis soon, and... you could die and leave me a single mom! And you're asking if it's *worth* it? Come on, Mark. Wake up!"

Jeffrey tried to smooth things over. "Tell Tamara we'll find him. I'll hire a PI." He paused, tapping his fingers on his desk. "But Tamara, what you need to understand is… for some reason, Eric was angry. At us, at the world. And angry people aren't apt to help others. Let's not get our hopes up."

Jeffrey sat across from Darren Townsend at the Dupont Coffee Shop not far from the Dupont Circle Metro Station. He had given the private investigator all the information that he had on Eric; from where he had lived once he got out of jail–at least until recently–to his social security number and most recent cell phone number.

"The photos are a bit outdated–as I said, I haven't even talked to Eric in the past few years."

Darren waved him off. "Not a problem. I'll get one from the Maryland Department of Motor Vehicles. I've got a contact there. I just need to verify that whatever is on file there is the real deal."

"Any idea how long this might take?"

Darren shrugged, but not unsympathetically. "Look," he said in his mild Australian accent. "I'll find him. No guarantees–that wouldn't be ethical–but your son doesn't sound like he's a professional at disappearing. And I even find those that're pros. So while I can't promise, I do believe that it's going to be a short time–like a day or two."

Jeffrey forced a smile. "Thanks. Great. As I said, money's no object."

"Dr. Coleman, money is always an object. And an important one at that." The investigator stretched his hands in front of him, slowly clasping fingers and cracking his knuckles. "But I understand your urgency, and I don't charge more for doing my job well. All I ask is that you refer me to any friends or colleagues who might need a trustworthy investigator. Once you're satisfied with my results, of course."

"Of course."

They shook hands and Darren promised to call, then Jeffrey called Tamara and told her about the meeting.

"Just make sure he doesn't screw you around," she said. "I'm worried about Mark. Every time he coughs, I panic. I feel like... "

"I know, Tamara. But, again, please understand that finding him may be the easy part. He may not talk to me, let alone volunteer a kidney."

"Well, that's where you earn your keep as a parent," Tamara said, with an icy edge to her voice. "Just make it happen."

Chapter Seven

"Take a look at this," said Louise, pointing at her computer screen.

Darren was impressed. "Have you found him already?"

"Just an address. But that's a pretty good place to start. I don't think he was making any real attempt to go underground. His SSN was there for anyone to find."

"Good job."

"Wish they were all this easy!" she grinned. "Give me your iPhone. I'll program directions to his apartment into your Google maps."

Darren squinted at the screen. "Randolph Road in Rockville? Don't bother, I know that area well. Geez, talk about hiding in plain sight! The client–his father–lives just a few miles away in Bethesda." He scribbled down the address. "Wish me luck."

Darren drove down the Rockville Pike, passing the White Flint shopping mall. He was anxious to complete this job, because he knew that every satisfied customer always meant referrals to new customers. But it seemed as though the traffic conspired against him, as he hit nearly every red light heading north. Finally he signaled east on Randolph Road and soon found himself turning left into a large and well-kept apartment complex opposite a strip mall containing a Safeway, bank and several other stores. The area verged on the industrial side, with a U-Haul rental place behind the complex and a gas station kitty-corner, but seemed to border on a tree-lined brownstone neighborhood to the northeast. Looking at his iPhone map, Darren realized that they must be fairly close to the Rock Creek Park that connected Lake Needwood to Georgetown in DC.

Parking his truck, Darren wandered over to one of the entrances, glancing at the apartment numbers to see which entrance was the right one. In this building alone, there were about five different entrances, each with a staircase going up to the second floor. And the entire U-shaped complex had at least three different brick buildings. He found the entrance with numbers that matched the address given to him by Louise and climbed to the second floor. The door stood on the left, but there was no name on the door. There wasn't even a welcome mat on the floor in front of the door. He decided to have a closer look at the mailbox before knocking—he wanted as much evidence as possible that it was really Eric Coleman living there before confronting the man—and went back down the stairs. Sure enough, there was a little typed sign that said E. Coleman on the mailbox. But the mailbox was stuffed with papers and envelopes, and Darren had a sinking feeling that his target was either away from his apartment, or not checking his mail.

Back in front of the door, Darren took a deep breath and knocked. Nothing. There was an almost hollow sound that echoed from inside, which Darren didn't find particularly encouraging. As the seconds ticked into a couple minutes without any response to his repeated knocking and ringing of the bell, he began to have doubts as to whether Eric was home—or even still living in the apartment. If he had been in a first floor apartment rather than up the flight of stairs, Darren would have moseyed around to the other side and had a little peek into the sliding glass window that led out to the grassy common area. Upstairs, however, there were little balconies, and he knew that without equipment and backup it was too dangerous to climb up the drainpipe for a look.

What to do? Darren was not impetuous, which was one of the reasons that he was such a professional and highly respected PI. The neighbor across the hall might know something, but the resident apartment complex manager was the real best bet. And Darren worried that the neighbor might become suspicious and call the manager—and that would make it next to impossible to get any information out of the manager after that. He'd be pissed off at Darren right from the start. And unlike the neighbor, who may or may not know something of value, the manager would know for certain if Eric had given notice, or was just out of town or away for a few days. Or he could be dead? Was it possible? Could he be lying dead inside the apartment? Darren calculated that there must be at least four days of mail piled up in his box. It wasn't likely; the entire entrance would be reduced to a horrible stench if that were the case. No, he must be away–temporarily or permanently–Darren needed to find out.

Talking with the manager, however, presented some problems. Building managers weren't lawyers–otherwise they wouldn't be living in a little apartment taking care of maintenance issues. But in his experience, both professionally and as an apartment renter, those guys had a lot of legal knowledge. They worked hand in hand with property lawyers, and knew all about respecting the privacy of residents. It was surprising, Darren thought–most people were used to TV style PIs, full of blaggery and smooth-talking trickery. Yet, when push came to shove, he knew that often honesty was the best policy. Even if in some cases there were parts of that honesty that might have to be omitted. All for the good of the client, of course.

Darren walked over to the first building where there was a little sign that said *Manager* and rang the bell. A tall man in his mid-thirties opened the door and said, "Can I help you?"

Darren introduced himself, and shook hands with the man, who said his name was Allan Cook. Darren looked around the little office, which had been converted from an apartment, and was furnished with a desk and computer, mesh office chair behind the desk, and two simpler chairs for visitors. There was also a sofa against the north wall with a large black cat sprawled on it.

Explaining his mission, Darren told Allan that he had found evidence that Eric was living here, in this complex–and that the mailbox had the correct name on it.

"Sorry. You probably know that I can't confirm or deny that there's anyone here by that name. You'd need a court warrant or police warrant for me to be able to pass out that kind of information."

Darren sighed. "I know. Your residents deserve their privacy. But this is a very unusual case. Let me give you some background. This isn't some scam, and it's not that Eric owes any money or anything. It's his own father who's looking for him."

He outlined the most pertinent details, and finished by admitting to Allan that Dr. Coleman, the father, didn't even know whether finding Eric would help. In fact, he was somewhat pessimistic that Eric would even be willing to talk to his dad at all, not to mention donate a kidney to his twin brother. As he revealed the story, he could see that Allan was moved–he could also tell that Allan knew something that he wasn't telling. Darren had a built-in BS sensor, and could easily pick out when people were lying. It was pretty simple; their eye contact was weak or different, they had little facial tics, and they had some internal discomfort that Darren could almost always pick up on. Except for the pathological liars who were always comfortable in their own skins. Those were tough to breach. But here, although Allan wasn't saying anything about Eric, he could tell that Allan knew something.

"So, can you help us out? We're talking about potentially saving a life."

Allan looked down at his shoes. "I'd like to help, but really... " he muttered.

"C'mon. I know he's either living here or did until recently. Eric hasn't even taken steps to hide it."

Allan looked everywhere but at Darren. "Well, how do I know that his father really sent you? I mean, I'd like to believe you. You seem like a reasonable guy. But I could get sued for releasing private information." He finally looked up. "How do I know you're not with those guys that are threatening him? The same guys who vandalized my car?"

Darren was puzzled by that last question, but this was the opportunity that he had been pushing for the past 25 minutes and he wasn't going to get side-tracked. At least not right now. "You are absolutely right, Allan, and I respect that. Here." He opened his briefcase and took out a signed letter from Dr. Jeffrey Coleman, printed on NIH letterhead.

Allan scanned the letter, seeing the *To whom it may concern*, and the statement that PI Darren Townsend was acting in his interests to find his son, in the hopes that he would be willing to donate a kidney that would save the life of his other son. Darren gave Allan his own driver's license and PI license, and a copy of Jeffrey Coleman's Maryland license. He saw the lines on Allan's face relax.

"Okay, okay." He ran his fingers through his thinning hair. "Eric Coleman was a resident here. Is a resident here. About four days ago, he had to call for an ambulance to come get him. I wasn't here, but my assistant told me that they took him to Georgetown Hospital."

"Drugs?"

"I don't know. Like I said, I wasn't here."

"What did you say about... people threatening him?"

Allan shook his head. "Beats me. It looked like a couple of thugs. They started out being really polite to me. Just like you." He offered a thin-lipped smile. "But when I wouldn't give them any information, they hinted that this apartment complex might not be in such a safe neighborhood."

"You didn't get any identifying information, driver's licenses or anything?"

"No, no. They wouldn't give them to me. But I filed a report with the police."

"You did? Why?"

Allan bit down on his lower lip. "They slashed my tires that night. Or at least it must have been them–I didn't actually see them."

"So you have no idea what they were looking for?"

"No."

"All I can say," said Darren, "is that I'm pretty sure they weren't after his kidney. Maybe other body parts, but definitely not kidneys."

Darren entered his office glumly and tossed his coat over one of the visitor chairs. Louise looked up at him cautiously, but he remained silent.

"Well?" she prompted.

"Well," he said. "Well, well, well. Goddamn well."

"I gather he wasn't at the apartment."

"No fooling, mate," Darren said. "But I did find him."

"And?"

He slumped into the other chair opposite her desk in the anteroom. "It's almost like the joke you Yanks always make. I've got good news and bad news–what do you want to hear first?"

"Just tell me what's going on!"

"We've definitely found our man. Without a doubt, it's Eric Coleman, the twin and owner of two kidneys, one of which is in great demand by his father and brother."

"And the bad news?"

Darren sighed, feeling for his client, and his frustration echoed off the office walls. "He's been hospitalized in the Georgetown Hospital dialysis unit–in the Division of Nephrology and Hypertension–for the last four days. It seems as though he's got kidney problems of his own to worry about. And–there seem to be some rather unsavory types who are also looking for him."

Chapter Eight

As Jeffrey climbed up the stairs to the Division of Nephrology and Hypertension at Georgetown Hospital, his thoughts spun around his head like foam in a whirlpool. It was less than an hour since he had met with Darren—who hadn't wanted to give him the news over the phone—and here he was, back at Georgetown Hospital again. Without Mark and Tamara.

On top of all of his other troubles, Jeffrey could not manage to tuck away the other information that Darren had bestowed on him: that someone else—or more accurately, "someones" in plural—were also desperately searching for Eric. This could only mean one thing, Jeffrey knew, and it was definitely related to drugs or drug money. Appreciative of Darren's quick results, he'd given him another retainer to find out who was after Eric, and why.

Taking the steps two at a time, he felt as if the world was caving in on him—again. Two years since Annie died, and he'd thought that nothing could ever be as bad. How could it possibly be? Both of his sons, his and Annie's twins, sick with Polycystic Kidney Disease? It was impossible to fathom, simply unbelievable. Yet, as a scientist, he knew that it made sense. After all, they were identical twins, carrying the very same DNA. Not 99.99% similar, as the rest of mankind was, or merely carrying half of his exact DNA as each child carried his or her parents' DNA. No, they were that extremely rare case among humankind, where each twin was genetically identical to the other. So while Eric might be a perfect genetic match for Mark to donate a kidney, it should have occurred to Jeffrey that Eric might be equally susceptible to Polycystic Kidney Disease.

Jeffrey approached the nurse at the station, and she accompanied him into the dialysis unit. It was a comfortably furnished room, with chairs that were a combination of hospital bed, dental chair and reclining chair set in a U in a room filled with high tech equipment. At the moment, only two of the chairs were manned, and Jeffrey easily recognized Eric despite his three-day beard stubble. He had a battalion of needles and tubes hooked and radiating from his arm, and he was leafing through a copy of *Sports Illustrated*. Jeffrey nodded to the nurse, and she adjusted a few dials for the other dialysis patient before heading back to her station outside the room.

Jeffrey took a deep breath. He wasn't sure what to say; in his head, he hadn't gotten to this part, and hadn't planned anything. So he went over and said, "Hi, Eric."

Darren Townsend watched as Jeffrey parked his car in the Georgetown Hospital lot. He and Louise had spent a lot of time strategizing, and although he hated to invade the privacy of a client—especially a good paying one who he felt was a genuinely nice guy—he saw no other way to home in on the trail of the men who were looking for Eric.

He had no doubt that these were gang members, and based on Eric's background, he strongly suspected that they were either after stolen drugs or drug money—something Eric had probably hidden away. This meant that he had to be particularly careful, because he knew that human life had little meaning for people like that. He shook his head, wondering how humanity had bred people for whom death had no meaning—who had no capacity for empathy. Drugs, he thought. Addictions that were so strong that everything else became irrelevant.

He watched Jeffrey lock his car and hurry toward the hospital entrance, shoulders slumped slightly and body bent forward, like a runner trying to hit the tape. He knew that Jeffrey would be anxious to see his son—and he was counting on the fact that the thugs looking for Eric also knew that Jeffrey would lead them to his son.

Although Darren had not been able to pick out a specific vehicle tailing Jeffrey in the heavy DC traffic—after all, he had his work cut out for him just making sure that neither Jeffrey nor anyone tailing him would notice that he too was following Jeffrey—

he was reasonably certain that the thugs would have Jeffrey in their sights. They weren't stupid. Well, that wasn't accurate–they were, otherwise why would they be gang members and drug runners? What he meant, he corrected himself, was that he shouldn't underestimate them. They knew what they were doing. Underestimating bad guys was something that he knew could get him killed, and while Darren was not the type to back down, he knew the value of being cautious. No point getting hurt–he had to pay for his own medical coverage.

He called Louise and updated her. "I'm watching the door. I'll update you if I see anything."

"Got it."

No sooner had Darren clicked off than two men got out of a parked blue Ford Escort in the opposite corner of the lot. It was not the type of car Darren would have associated with gangbangers, but perhaps they were getting smarter. No more black Trans Ams or cars with long tail pipes and ostentatious decals. No, they were into non-descript cars for their day-to-day business.

Despite their clothes–not jean jackets or grey hoodies, but sport coats and loafers–Darren could smell them a mile away. The cocky way the driver clicked his door locked, and the silent but meaningful flick of his partner's head toward Jeffrey's Prius. Darren had his binoculars clipped to the camera of his iPhone. This little custom connector was a technological marvel. He had learned this trick after a trip to Costa Rica the previous winter when he had gone on bird watching excursions, and saw the guides all set their tripods and binoculars and used them to take pictures on the smart phones of the people in the group. Darren, who immediately realized the potential of such technology for his line of work, had come home and had his binoculars outfitted so that his iPhone fit right on. Since then, he had increased his range and resolution for taking photos and videos, and the technology had served him well.

Darren was filming as the two men approached Jeffrey's car. Darren could see that there was no one around–except for him–and he knew that the thugs had not seen him. He held his breath as the pair of them pulled out nine-inch blades and slashed all four of Jeffrey's tires. The driver then pulled out what looked like a small hammer and then proceeded to smash all of the windows. There was surprisingly little noise as he did this, and it was further masked by the deep voluntary coughs the man made each time just as he slammed the hammer into the windshield.

Darren called Louise back and reported the events quietly to Louise on the phone. "I'm hanging back and catching this on film. Perhaps I should go and bust those low lifes."

"No, Dare. Just get a vid. Much more useful."

"I know," he replied, kicking the inside of his car door lightly in frustration. "It's just, sometimes it would be great to catch them in the act and teach them a lesson."

He knew that although he could have intervened and prevented the damage, that it was only property, and it was probably better to let them do their worst and capture it all on film. If he had stopped them–aside from potentially getting hurt–they would have just done their damage at another time in another place. This was the opportunity to catch them in the act and put them away. If not for drugs, at least for vandalism.

"Stay cool, Dare."

Louise always had his back, Darren thought. If he hadn't known that she was a lesbian, he would have thought that she had a crush on him. But it was good that she didn't–at least in the romantic sense. That's why they made such a great team. There was no sexual tension between them, just trust.

"They're going in, Lou. Call the cops, tell 'em about the car. I've gotta make sure our client and junior are ok."

"Okay."

Darren slid out of the car, pocketing the phone, and leaving the binoculars on the floor. Seeing the two vandals enter an empty elevator with no one else inside, Darren make a tactical decision not to get in with them. They were here for Eric, but trashing Jeffrey's car was probably an added perk for them.

Seeing the elevator stop on four and then slide back to three, Darren hit the stairs and bounded up two at a time. He smiled over at the nurse station, and his face lit up in a real smile when the young nurse smiled back. That old Aussie charm, he thought. Usually he had to open his mouth and let out some Crocodile Dundee charm, but this time it was easy. But then the two gangbangers had also got by. Huh, he thought. Maybe I'm not so special. But when he entered the dialysis room, he quickly became all business–and not a minute too soon.

Jeffrey was lying on the floor, holding his nose with blood gushing out. Darren noted that he looked dazed, but was probably going to be okay. Eric, on the other hand, was getting worked over. One thug had shoved a sock in his mouth and was wrapping duct tape over the sock, from ear to ear. The other had just finished tying his hands and was calmly pulling out the needles from Eric's veins. As he ripped out each needle, Darren saw Eric's eyelids flutter and his eyes bulge out in pain.

Whispering into his headset from the edge of the doorway, Darren said, "Lou, make sure the cops get up to the fourth floor, pronto. I think they're trying to abduct Eric Coleman from the dialysis unit. Father is semi-conscious on the floor—get an ambu—I mean, get the docs over here with the cops. I'm gonna act now."

"Be careful!"

In less than a second, Darren assessed the situation. He liked being his own boss now, but his time in Australia's special force Tactical Assault Group, also known as TAG, was well spent. The thug disconnecting Eric from the machines was a step closer, with the added advantage that his back was fully to the door. Before the man even knew he was there, Darren grabbed his arm, twisted it around and dislocated his shoulder. As he cried out and turned to face his attacker, Darren kicked his left knee with a side-kick, effectively disabling him. At least until after he had his meniscus surgically repaired.

The second thug turned away from Eric and reached into his pocket. With the element of surprise gone, Darren knew that now things might be a little trickier. Although he was licensed to carry a gun in Maryland and DC, Darren believed that his weapon was best situated in his safe. In fact, all people's weapons were best situated there. Besides, in his line of work, one needed to be able to get in and out of places in a hurry, and toting a weapon around was not practical. Even now, as the thug pulled out the hammer that he had used to smash the car windows, Darren knew that he didn't need a gun. He was close enough for hand-to-hand combat, and a weapon was unnecessary.

Darren took a step forward. "Put the hammer down. Your mate isn't going very far, and even if you get away, he'll grass on you." Darren could never resist using Brit-speak with these types of goons. The man just sneered and waved the hammer menacingly, so Darren added, "C'mon, mate. You don't want to get hurt, do you?"

As the man was winding up to heave the hammer at Darren's head, Darren lunged forward and closed the gap—until there was nowhere left to throw the hammer. Darren kneed him in the groin, and as he connected, the guy went "Uuumph!" Darren spun him around and knocked his feet out from under him. "Hey Lou, it's over—two strikes. Are the cops coming, or do I have to tie up these bozos?"

"Should be there any sec, Dare. You all right?"

"Never better. They don't make bad guys like they used to. I see the security and cops are coming. Gotta go see if the Colemans are okay."

Forty minutes later, Jeffrey again stood in front of his son. Darren had helped Jeffrey up and had gotten his nose looked at by one of the doctors on the ward, and Eric had been hooked back up to the dialysis machine. Jeffrey thanked Darren profusely, although he was upset to learn that he no longer had a drivable vehicle.

"I'll check in with you later. I'm off to the police station to make a statement and sign some papers," Darren said.

"Okay. Thank you again."

Eric Coleman watched the man who had probably saved his life leave, and then looked up at his father, who was holding a cloth and still mopping a little blood from his nose. And then he looked away quickly. At the ceiling. At the floor. Anywhere but in Jeffrey's direction.

"Hey," Jeffrey tried again.

"What do you want?" Eric barely mumbled out of the corner of his mouth. "Isn't it enough to have guys who want to kidnap or kill me?"

This wasn't going to be easy, Jeffrey thought. "How're you feeling?"

"What do you care? You never did."

Rather than get in an argument about who was unfair to whom, Jeffrey reckoned his energies would be better focused on the present. "I'm told it was touch-and-go for awhile when the ambulance brought you in."

Eric acknowledged the statement with a minimal nod.

"Is it painful?"

Eric nodded again.

"Eric," Jeffrey began. "I know we've not seen eye to eye on many things–"

"Eye to eye?" Eric sat upright in his chair. "Who are you kidding? Even as a kid I knew Mark was your favorite." He let the air out of his lungs. "At least Mom didn't treat me like dog shit."

"Look, Eric. I'll accept some of the blame. Perhaps not all of it–there's still some responsibility you have to take–but can't we put this behind us for now? Aren't there more important things in the future to concern us?"

Eric shook his head with determination. "I'm not stupid, you know. Maybe not as smart as Markie-boy, but I read. I know the statistics: kids with screwed up childhoods always turn out lousy. So you're responsible for the way I ended up."

"Alright, Eric. For convenience sake now, let's suppose I'm responsible. But now I want to make it up to you. Can you let it go?"

Eric stroked his chin and then said, "Okay, cut me a check for twenty grand."

Jeffrey stared at him in disbelief. "What?"

Eric continued. "You were the one who said you wanted to make it up to me. Prove it. Write me a check for 20K. You saw what those SOBs tried to do to me–if I don't pay them off, they'll kill me. This is only the beginning."

Jeffrey couldn't believe his ears. His own son was blackmailing him, asking him to pay $20,000 so that he would forgive him for transgressions that Jeffrey knew were largely in Eric's head. And yet, he so badly wanted to make peace with his son, especially as he was hooked up to a dialysis machine.

Jeffrey pulled his checkbook out of his pocket, scrawled on a check, tore it out of the booklet and handed it to Eric. Jeffrey watched Eric's face slowly transform from that mask of anger to a very slow grin. Finally, Eric said, "Well, that's more like it. Alright, we're even for now."

Jeffrey clasped Eric's free hand, struggling to avoid tearing up, and asked again. "How're you feeling?"

Eric seemed torn between self-pity and bravado, but the bravado won out and he replied, "Now might be a good time to take out a life insurance policy on me, Dad."

Sitting down on a regular chair beside him, Jeffrey asked, "How long have you been in the hospital?"

"Four days." The bravado was gone altogether. "I've been feeling really shitty for awhile. Since I, you know, got out. Bad pain in my lower back, and I've been pissing blood. I was sorta hoping it was an infection or something, and would just go away."

A nurse came in and they were silent while she took Eric's blood pressure and vitals, checked the dials on the machines, and finally retreated from the room.

Eric continued. "Dad, believe me, I was going to call you–I mean, I really was."

Jeffrey nodded, not knowing what else to say.

"No, Dad, I see you don't believe me, but I had a tip–you know, for the stock market." He looked away. "I just wanted to be a success, to do something that you would appreciate. So you'd be proud of me. But then this happened."

Jeffrey listened as Eric described how he had managed to call 911, despite the pain. How the paramedics had carted him to the hospital. The meeting with Dr. Williams, the nephrologist who diagnosed him with Polycystic Kidney Disease, and the grim prognosis.

"Dad, I need a kidney transplant, as soon as possible. The doctor says that this dialysis may keep me alive for a few months, but that I need a kidney if I want to reach my next birthday." His eyes welled up with tears. "I know I haven't been a model son–or brother. But will you help me?"

Examining the email that had just come through, Jeffrey felt a wave of frustration and the beginning of a migraine working its way through his skull. The critiques from the review of Jai's manuscript had just been sent to him, and he had to ball his fists to avoid from throwing his laptop at the wall. Two reviewers had essentially voiced acceptance of the manuscript, noting that they had no further concerns and that the study made important advances in the field. The third reviewer, just as he had the previous round–and this time Jeffrey was certain that the anonymous reviewer was, of course, Rob Danfield–had outlined an additional new long series of experiments that he absolutely insisted needed to be done before the manuscript could be properly evaluated. There was no doubt, thought Jeffrey, that Danfield was abusing his trust as a reviewer of their paper to delay or reject it–so that his own manuscript would be accepted first. That was the problem in science–you were either first, or you were no one.

So what to do? The editor who was handling Jeffrey's manuscript had accepted the premise of Danfield's "expert" opinion, and had written to Jeffrey that he could not, in good conscience, accept the manuscript with so many serious flaws, and that for Jeffrey to have his manuscript accepted, it would require significant additional experimentation.

Picking up his phone, Jeffrey speed-dialed Jai. "I just forwarded the new editor's decision and critiques to you Jai–we need to talk."

"What did the editor say?"

Sighing, Jeffrey outlined the editor's decision and briefed Jai on the problems with the one reviewer. "Let's discuss this over coffee–Lilit on Old Georgetown?"

"I'm on my way," said Jai.

Sipping his cappuccino across from Jai, who in addition to his coffee had ordered a sumptuous-looking gelato, Jeffrey began pensively. "We have to figure out what we should do."

By now Jai had read the critiques closely, and he shook his head. "Jeffrey, if we try to do these experiments, revise and resubmit again, they'll scoop us. This guy isn't going to let our paper get accepted–we'll do everything he asked for, and he'll keep asking for new experiments, or just say that the paper doesn't provide a big enough advance to warrant publication."

"But what if we do all these experiments and then I write the editor a letter outlining how we have *twice* done whatever this reviewer has asked for, and satisfied the concerns of both other reviewers? Then I could ask for a new, neutral, fourth reviewer, to get another impression of our study?"

"You know that Danfield is determined to slow us down. The journal respects its reviewers, and the editor would be unlikely to go against Danfield if he is adamant." Jai spooned up some gelato. "We need to try something else."

Jeffrey was conscious that to some extent, his role as Jai's mentor had reversed, and Jai was now playing the role of the responsible adult. He was having trouble keeping his family and health issues from interfering with his efficiency at work, and found himself relying more and more on his younger colleague's judgment. "Do you have anything in mind?"

"That's why I have the gelato," said Jai, pointing to his head. "The sugar rush to my brain has given me an idea."

"Well," said Jeffrey, "what is it?"

Leaning back in his chair, Jai said, "My brother Alok, the one who is a programming engineer, may be able to help."

"How?"

"You've of course heard of computer viruses and worms, eh?"

"Sure. But what have they to do with our paper?"

"Well, Alok has been working on an experimental louse that might be useful."

Jeffrey scratched his head involuntarily. "A louse?"

"It's like a worm, but the idea is that it creates a system of binary integers that are embedded in the CPU, and they…"

Jeffrey held up a hand. "Let's keep this simple. Worm, virus, louse. Okay. What does that have to do with our study?"

"Alok has experimented with a new garage door, basically a way of getting the louse onto someone's computer and obtaining the data on that system. And Alok has a good friend in IT at UCSF. It would be easy for him to get the *louse* onto Danfield's system via the garage door. And Alok is a pro—nobody would ever know, and even if some crack super-cyber-team ever found the louse—which they wouldn't—there would be no way to track it back to Alok or anyone."

Jeffrey frowned, not liking the idea of lice and garage doors—especially the illegal implications involved in such a plan. After all, he was a government employee, with a guaranteed pension. Why would he endanger all that to get some kind of vigilante justice? On the other hand, he thought bitterly, Annie was gone, both of his sons were sick with Polycystic Kidney Disease—was there really much left for him to lose?

"Let me get this straight," he said slowly, "what you're proposing, Jai, is that we illegally obtain all of Danfield's data from his computer—and then what? We alter his data to trip him up? I can't do that—that's really wrong."

Jai smiled and his head bobbed in that familiar Indian gesture that Jeffrey had come to know so well. He had once thought it meant "no," because it involved a certain degree of the lateral head movement that in most western countries usually signified the negative. But over time he came to understand that this was agreement. Despite himself, Jeffrey smiled inwardly and thought how interesting it was that while a smile—which required the control of many facial muscles—universally signified happiness, the direction on which one moved one's head was not a universal signal.

Jeffrey floated back from his reverie to find that Jai was still talking. "...it's just that in the case of Danfield, he really deserves it."

Taking back his role as the responsible mentor, Jeffrey said, "No, Jai. I draw the line there. We won't do anything like that. No fabricating or altering data." But as he watched Jai's face crumble, he added, "But I think I have an idea of what we might be able to do."

Jeffrey pulled a second beer out of the fridge, popped it open and took a long chug. The alcohol, already at one beer more than his usual self-imposed limit, was not helping him think. Vi, who despite her sixty plus pounds had a self-image of a lap dog, climbed all over him and did everything except drink his beer. In an atypical demonstration of frustration, he scolded her, "Get down—off," and shooed her away. She sat in the corner of the living, sulking at the banishment from her human and favorite chair. But Jeffrey was in no mood to appease her.

What the hell was he going to do? What would he say to Mark and Tamara? He wasn't sure how Mark would take it—he had never really expressed any optimism that his twin might be likely to donate a kidney. But Tamara would be livid. It was just too sickening to be true; not only had she insisted that he find and contact Eric, to see if a perfect kidney match could be found—but now she would find out that she had sent her father-in-law on a worse-than-fool's-errand. Eric not only wouldn't be donating a kidney, but he would be needing one, and even sooner than Mark.

Jeffrey tightened his scarf around his neck and shivered. It was cold and damp, as it often was in the DC area, but the wind made it especially uncomfortable. Why was it that bad news always had to be passed on in miserable weather? Annie's diagnosis had been relayed by her doctor on a cold December day; there had even been a dusting of snow.

He climbed up the flight of steps to his son's apartment, bracing himself as he went. He had struggled during the car ride, trying to get every word right, but he knew that unlike the professional science seminars that he was routinely invited to deliver, all bets were off as to what he would actually say once inside the apartment. His heart was pounding as he rang the bell.

"Dad! What are you doing here?"

Before he could answer, he heard Tamara calling from the kitchen: "Mark, who is it?"

"It's just Dad," Mark answered. He glanced at his father in some embarrassment. "I mean, it's not *just* dad, it's just that I didn't expect... Oh, never mind. Let me take your coat."

Tamara came out of the kitchen. "Hi. We just finished dinner. Would you like a cup of coffee?"

"That would be great."

As they settled down at the tiny kitchen table, Tamara measured out water and ground coffee. "I gather it's still too early to hear anything from that investigator?"

The best-laid plan, thought Jeffrey as he looked down at his shoes. He had hoped to bring it out at his own pace. Well here goes. He looked over the counter at Tamara and back to Jeffrey. "The PI was very fast. He did find Eric."

Tamara lost all interest in the coffee preparation and sat down beside Mark. "And? Did you see him? What did he say?"

Mark looked stricken, and worry lines framed his forehead. "Dad, you did your best–I know you did–if he said no, we understand."

Tamara broke in. "No, Mark. We do *not* 'understand.' That would be entirely unacceptable. Jeffrey, you need to convince him. End of story. This isn't some little family squabble any more. Blood is thicker than water, and a good person would save the life of a perfect stranger, not to mention a twin brother. What's so complicated about that?"

Mark tried to defend his father. "Tamara, Dad's always done his best with Eric, it's just—"

"Mark, be quiet." Tamara clenched her teeth. "You are not going to get bullied all your life." She pointed at Jeffrey. "If you won't go back and talk to him, persuade him to do this, then I will. Give me his number."

"Tamara," Jeffrey started, "there's—"

"If he won't listen," Tamara cut him off, "we'll pay him. Lots of money. My parents would be willing to chip in, I'm sure of it."

Jeffrey had known that this would be hard, but even the prelude was turning out to be more difficult than he had anticipated. He held up his hands. "That's not the problem. It's much worse than an issue of convincing him."

Jeffrey could tell that Mark's brain was in overdrive, and his son asked, "Where did you find him, Dad? Or rather, where did the PI find him?"

With a sigh, Jeffrey said, "The Georgetown Hospital Division of Nephrology and Hypertension Dialysis Unit." He watched as Mark slowly nodded, and as the ramifications sank in, Tamara emitted a gasp. So far he had given them bad news. He would soon follow that with terrible news. His heart went out to the young couple, with their lives supposedly ahead of them.

"He's got it, too?" Tamara asked, stunned.

Jeffrey hung his head. "I'm sorry. I should have thought that there was a real possibility that he'd also have PKD, but it just didn't occur to me."

Without a word, Mark stood and put the coffee on. Jeffrey explained how Darren Townsend had tracked Eric down and pulled the information on Eric's collapse and transport by ambulance to the hospital.

"So Dad, what did you do?" Mark asked eventually. "Just waltz into the dialysis unit and say 'Hi Eric,' what's up?' Can't imagine he was too happy to see you."

Jeffrey counted to three in his head. "I walked over and he recognized me."

Now it was Tamara's turn to be cynical. "He recognized you. Gee golly darn, what a great son. How wonderful." She looked over the counter at Mark. "But who cares. I guess it's back to square one. We follow Dr. Jergen's plan—hope and wait for a perfect donor

67

match, but we do it knowing that we've always got your dad here as a backup if things suddenly get worse—or if they can't find you a better match."

Mark was nodding, but Jeffrey couldn't manage to look at either of them. He saw them look at each other, and Tamara went on the attack. "What? Jeffrey, what is it? What's going on? What are you hiding?"

Feeling like a monster, Jeffrey gripped the edge of the table. He didn't even bother telling them about his run-in with the thugs and their attempt to abduct Eric; he just stuck with the parts that had a bearing on Mark. "Eric's on dialysis for a reason. I spoke to the doctor, and his situation is critical."

"Yeah," Tamara said. "So what are they planning?"

Jeffrey could see that neither of them had internalized what the situation meant, and this made it all the more difficult. "Guys, Eric has terminal kidney disease. He's only alive because of the dialysis—and even that may be temporary, if he doesn't get a transplant. Soon. Otherwise the doctor says he could die."

The room was silent, and Jeffrey could hear the steady ticking of the clock on the wall. Nobody moved. He could sense their incomprehension—or at least their unwillingness to acknowledge what was to come next. They were making him spell it out, point by point, and each detail that he was forced to share felt like a nail being hammered into his chest.

"So," Mark finally broke the silence. "What's going to happen?"

"Mark... you know I would do absolutely anything for you. I want you to understand this, because I need to save Eric's life—I need to donate a kidney to him. Right away."

Mark froze, but Tamara leapt to her feet. "You are going to give *him* a kidney? Are you crazy? He hates you, he's ignored you for the past 10 years, and you would rather save *his* life than Mark's?" She shook her head in disgust. "Jeffrey, I don't believe you'd do that to Mark! To us!"

Jeffrey looked away. "Tamara. Mark. I'm not doing this to harm you. You've got to understand how difficult a situation this is." He spread his hands out on the table. "He's at the end of the road—he needs a kidney *now*. If he doesn't get one, he's going to have multiple organ failure and die. The dialysis is barely keeping him alive." He closed his eyes and then opened them. "You, on the other hand, are in much better shape. Not on dialysis. You could easily survive a year or longer if things go well until another donor surfaces. I can't stand by and watch Eric die."

Mark nodded in understanding, but Tamara would not be appeased. "So you're going to gamble with Mark's life? You're going to assume that he'll be fine, until we get a donor? *If* we get a donor!" She turned to Mark. "I just can't believe what I'm hearing!"

Almost as though it was someone else's life on the line, Mark said, "Dad, can't you just wait a few weeks—maybe even a month or two? I mean, if I knew I had a matched kidney, it wouldn't be a problem." He looked pleadingly at Jeffrey.

"Mark, I can't wait. His doctor says that he may only have weeks, or even days to live." Looking ten years older, he slowly shook his head. "I just can't sit by and watch that happen when I can prevent it. He's still my son."

Tamara was about to cut in, but Mark put up his hand to stop her. "You are sacrificing my life, and the father of your grandchild for someone who is only technically your son. Face it, he couldn't have cared less if you dropped off the face of the earth. But I bet he's nice to you now that you're a donor."

"Mark, he's dying. At least until a kidney transplant takes." Feeling the muscles tight in his back, Jeffrey stood up, pushed back his chair and stretched. "People change when they face death. There are instances where drunks become sober when they receive a terminal diagnosis. Even cases of bipolar patients who appear to be cured. I think he's realized that life is too precious to waste. Whatever's left of it for him."

When they didn't reply, Jeffrey stood up and put his coat on. As he headed to the door Mark asked, "So is there a date set for harvesting your kidney and the transplant?"

"Next week. We don't have the exact day and time yet, but it's got to be soon or it'll be too late. Let's talk tomorrow—I need to get home to take Vi out before her bladder bursts."

As soon as Mark closed the door, Tamara grabbed him by the shoulders. "Mark, we've got to do something. This is… just… I can't believe he'd do that to us!"

"C'mon Tamara, he's not 'doing it to us.' He's just trying to save Eric's life."

"Yeah. Right. And what does that do to *us?* I'm not going to let it happen. We need his kidney as a backup. What if you don't get a donor in time? Don't you get it?" Tamara was shouting now. "We're not talking about career choices and lifestyles–we're talking about staying as a family, or you dying on me! No, no–I'm going to talk to your dad tomorrow. No way I'm going to let this happen!"

Chapter Nine

Tamara grabbed her bag and headed out the door. All throughout her shift that morning she had managed to contain her rage, but she could feel it percolating and ready to boil over at any moment. As she descended the long escalator down to the Metro, climbing down on the left side and impatiently calling out "Excuse me!" to anyone who dared stand on the left side without physically climbing down, she felt a certain power flow through her body. She was right–morally and logistically–and that made all the difference. Being right made it so much easier to win the argument. And that was exactly what she intended to do.

The Medical Center Metro Station was crowded as usual, and even by adding her own energy to that of the escalator, it took several minutes to get to the Visitor Center. She waited impatiently in line, pushed her bag through the X-ray scan and glared at the federal officer who had to pat her down because her belt had caused the metal detector to beep. She showed her driver's license and was given a day pass to enter the NIH. What a messed up world we live in, she thought–20 murderous hijackers in 2001, and now, more than ten years later, the innocent citizens at large were still paying the price.

She had been to Jeffrey's office and lab several times over the past few years, albeit with Mark leading the way, but she had a good sense of direction and easily navigated her way to his building. It was a cool day, yet she was dressed warmly and felt a tingle of sweat down her back as she entered his building. She was coming unannounced, because she did not want to give him any further opportunity to justify his stupid decision. She planned to storm into his office and essentially remain there until he changed his mind. When she reached his floor, she was surprised that the office was empty, and Jeffrey's name was gone. A woman in a white lab coat looked at her curiously and asked "May I help you?"

"I'm Jeffrey Coleman's daughter-in-law. His office used to be here?"

"Oh, Dr. Coleman—he's the new Branch Chief. Let me take you."

Tamara followed the woman through a maze of hallways into an anteroom where a secretary was typing rapidly on a keyboard. The woman in the lab coat said, "This is Dr. Coleman's daughter-in-law." She smiled at Tamara and went back the way she came.

The secretary, whose nametag said *Mary*, smiled up at her. "Hold on a moment, I'll see if he's free." She came back quickly and pointed toward a door behind her. "Go on back."

Tamara went in and said, "You have a new office?"

"It came with the new position. I was comfortable in the other office, but I need to have Mary nearby—without her, I couldn't manage this position." He motioned her to sit.

Although she had steeled herself for this confrontation, fueled by her anger and frustration at the injustice of life—and hit even harder by Jeffrey's decision to donate a kidney to Eric—when push came to shove, she just couldn't do it. He wasn't a bad man, or a cruel one. He loved his sons, and he had suffered terribly when his wife took sick and died. Spontaneous and completely unrehearsed, Tamara broke down into long, heart-throbbing sobs. "I'm sorry, I'm sorry, I'm sorry." She rocked back and forth in her chair, and Jeffrey came over and put an arm around her shoulder.

"I meant to come here and yell at you—to shake you out of your cocoon." Tears continued to flow down her cheeks. "I wanted to tell you how evil you are, how you may kill your only son who loves you, who even cares at all about you." She stopped and looked up at him. "But I can't. You are only doing what you think is best, even if it's the wrong choice."

"Tamara, I know that you're just looking out for Mark's best interests, but put yourself in my place. Think about it. Am I really doing the wrong thing? Do I really have a choice?"

Tamara nodded. "Yes, you do have a choice. And in your position, with a son like Eric who has never loved you, why would you favor him over the son who has always loved and respected you? The choices that Eric made over the years, that brought him to drugs, gambling, jail. Do you think they deserve consideration on your part? Above taking care of Mark?" She shook her head. "You're gambling with his life!"

Jeffrey sat back resignedly. He had never been particularly good at math, but here the equation was simple. One kidney to donate, and two sons who needed it to survive. No amount of calculus or linear algebra, or any other fancy theorem could possibly alter the reality on the ground. One kidney just wasn't going to cut it. What the hell was he supposed to do? He had witnessed Eric in the dialysis unit, struggling for his life, his proximity to the end—whereas with Mark, there was some time. How much time, no one could tell them. Would there be a donor in time to save him?

Watching Tamara wipe the tears from her face, he realized that she had a point. His decision had been made on the assumption that he owed each of his sons the same treatment. If the situation had been reversed—if it had been Mark who was in immediate need of a kidney and Eric who had PKD, but no definite timeline for requirement of a transplant—he would not have hesitated. If both sons were to be treated as equals, his decision was an ethically correct one. But if, as Tamara pointed out, Eric had defaulted on his being treated the same as Mark because of his behavior over the past fifteen years, was it still the right decision? Did he not owe his first loyalty to the son who had been there for him when Annie died? Where had Eric been? Selling drugs? Demanding money even as Annie lay dying in the hospice?

He recalled how Eric had phoned him, just three days before Annie had died. So wrapped up in his world of drugs and debts that he hadn't even asked about her. Not once in the conversation, until Jeffrey had finally been unable to contain his utter disdain, "Eric, are you planning to see your mom in the hospice? She might not have much time left."

He had been stunned at his reply. "I'll try, Dad. If you can get me that money, I might have more time and be able to come out and see her." And despite Jeffrey giving in and sending him a large sum of money, he had never showed up until the funeral. And even then he was late. "Tamara," he said abruptly, "I think you're right.

I'm going to go tell Eric that I can't go through with the donation to him. I'm sorry—it's just such an impossible situation."

Her tears turned to relief, and she was shaking all over as she stood. "Thank you. Oh thank you, I knew you would understand."

Jeffrey nodded solemnly to the station nurse, and continued on toward the hemodialysis room where Eric was in the midst of a five-hour dialysis. Peeking in, he saw his son with a vast network of tubing hooked up to his left arm. He supposed it was better than the peritoneal catheter that one of the other men in the room had. However, Eric did not look well: his skin had an unhealthy yellowish sheen, and the hair under his ball cap was oily and unwashed. It was hard to tell if he was physically in pain, but he certainly didn't look relaxed.

Unable to do it yet, Jeffrey kept walking and went into the men's room. Sweating profusely, although he wasn't warm, he splashed water on his face and looked in the mirror. *I look almost as bad as Eric.* Right away he felt guilty comparing their situations, and he looked away; taking a deep breath, he went back to the dialysis room.

Eric was still sleeping, although every few seconds he jerked his neck from side to side, as though following a ping-pong match. Jeffrey sat down, and not wanting to wake his son, pulled out a draft of Jai's manuscript and began to read. After about twenty minutes, he noticed that Eric's eyes were flickering, opening and closing rapidly, like the tongue of a lizard flicking this way and that. He waited patiently until Eric seemed to have his bearings, and then coughed gently. Startled, Eric looked toward him, but once he realized it was Jeffrey, a slow grin appeared on his face. "Hey, Dad, you scared the shit out of me. Are you trying to give me a heart attack so you don't have to give up your kidney?" He lifted his left arm. "Christ, I feel like a fucking sieve—they keep poking away at me, and my arm hurts like a motherfucker. Shit, sorry."

Too uncomfortable to say anything, Jeffrey just nodded. Eric took that as interest and continued. "I can't wait to get this shit out of my arm. They say the dialysis is only 10% as effective as a kidney, and maybe it's keeping me alive, but goddamn, everything hurts.

And I'm just so tired–like I just got off an acid trip–not that you'd know."

Jeffrey realized that there was no easy way to do this, and if he didn't say it, no one would step in and do it for him. "Eric," he began.

Suddenly, Jeffrey was thrown back in time to when his twins were just children. He and Annie had bought them matching bicycles–the same color–it must have been for Hanukkah. Something had ticked Eric off–he had gone ballistic, ran screaming up to his room. What was it?

Jeffrey scrambled to remember what had happened–yes–they had gift-wrapped the bicycles, he and Annie. And then they had each made a card with one of the twin's names on it. Oh, that was it–both he and Annie had made cards for Mark. They had gotten their wires crossed, and made two cards out to Mark, and none for Eric. But what was the big deal? They had given a bicycle to each child–it was only a... well, a clerical error. He and Annie had been horrified by the mistake, but they thought that Eric would quickly forget in the excitement of riding his new bike. It had been a very mild December, and he thought that they would go out and drive along the Crescent Trail.

When Eric ran screaming to his room, he had thought that it was just another bit of histrionics; another attention seeking scheme. Eric had been into that kind of behavior. But Eric hadn't surfaced from his room, and refused to come and eat dinner. Annie had had to take him a tray up to his room. Had that been the beginning of all the trouble? Such a silly little error–nothing done on purpose. Jeffrey didn't know.

Eric cut into his reverie. "Oh, yeah. The doc was gonna contact you about stepping up the transplant date. He said that they can't get my hypertension under control, and he doesn't want to risk heart problems or even a stroke. Like I'm some kinda old man–c'n you believe it?"

Jeffrey couldn't do it. He had to talk to Dr. Ramsay. If Eric was telling the truth–and for once he had no reason to doubt him–pulling out as a kidney donor now would be a death sentence for him. Yanking a tissue out of his pocket, Jeffrey faked blowing his nose to hide the tears welling up in his eyes and told Eric he'd see him later.

Jeffrey was exhausted as he put the car in drive and headed south toward Tamara and Mark's apartment. He was sick and tired of these unexpected visits to their apartment, each time either as the bearer of terrible news, or as a punching bag. What he wanted to do was to go home and lie flat on his bed and remove all thoughts from his brain. No, what he really wanted to do was something that he had done only once in his life—after Annie had died: go out to a bar, on foot from his apartment in Bethesda, and get plastered. Skunked. Smashed. Totaled. Shitfaced! But he needed to get through the next hour first—and doing that while being sober wasn't going to be easy.

How could he possibly leave Eric out to dry... or rather, to die? A father just couldn't do that kind of thing, no matter how much grief his son had given him. Even knowing in his heart of hearts that this was the right decision—the only moral one he could possibly choose, despite the risk to Mark—he was absolutely dreading the upcoming meeting. He wasn't sure who he was afraid of most: Tamara had that passionate and impulsive anger, coupled with her hormones and upcoming motherhood, and she was a formidable protector of Mark. But while Mark seemed more resigned to his fate, Jeffrey knew that underneath the exterior, he was extremely vulnerable and that a decision to give his kidney to Eric would be shattering to Mark. This was not going to be a particularly fun bit of news to share.

With a deep sense of déjà vu, and fearing this encounter more than anything else in his life, with the possible exception of his visit to the Georgetown Hospital earlier that afternoon, Jeffrey put his head down and climbed the stairs. He looked at the stick figures that Tamara had made to decorate their door, with *Mark* and *Tamara* written below the male and female icons, respectively. The Tamara figure had a cute round belly, indicating her pregnancy, as if announcing to the world that the Colemans were soon slated to become three. Thinking of the number three, he counted and then rapped on the wood.

As soon as Tamara opened the door and peered at her father-in-law's anguished face, she knew that something had happened. Abandoning all civilities, she said, "What? What is it? What's wrong?"

Jeffrey just stood there, almost as though he didn't hear her. Tamara became aggravated at the lack of response, and repeated in a louder voice, "What?"

Jeffrey remained standing at the entrance to the apartment, dismayed that he hadn't even entered and was already on the defensive. He said, "Is Mark home?"

Tamara shook her head impatiently. "No, he had to go out to pick up some groceries. Did you break the news to Eric at Georgetown?"

Jeffrey frowned and said, "Do you mind if I come in? I won't take long. I would have preferred to talk to you both, but I can't stay." He was still pining for an evening at the neighborhood bar, where he might lose himself and his troubles for a few hours. Maybe enough to get some sleep tonight.

Despite her reluctance to wait any longer for Jeffrey to spit it out, Tamara invited him in, but didn't take his coat and she didn't offer to make coffee. They sat opposite each other in the kitchen, and she watched as Jeffrey unzipped his coat, crossed and uncrossed his legs. She had a gut-wrenching suspicion that she knew what this was all about, and although she hoped that she was wrong, there was no way she was going to make it easy for Jeffrey. If he had any thoughts about leaving Mark in the lurch, she was going to make him feel like the world's worst father. Which he was. Or would be, if her suspicions were correct. But he couldn't. No way. It was impossible.

Jeffrey cleared his throat, but rather than prod, Tamara punished him with a warm encouraging smile. "Too bad Mark isn't home," she said, "but I'll pass on to him whatever you have to say." She was actually pleased that Mark was out. He was too soft and would have tried to make Jeffrey comfortable—even if Jeffrey had come to give him bad news. People who brought bad news needed to pay for it, she thought. Especially if they were more than just the messenger, as in this case. But she waited, still hoping that she was wrong.

Finally he blurted out, "I can't do it—I'm sorry."

Tamara noticed how he averted his eyes, looking first at the refrigerator, then the range, and finally the coffee machine. Was he actually seeing those appliances? She doubted it. He looked like he was in some other sphere altogether. "Can't do what? You've been phenomenal until now, tracking down Eric in the hope of getting a kidney for Mark. I can't tell you how much we both appreciate everything you are doing for him." She paused and even took his hand on the table. "Your decision to keep the kidney and wait to see if Mark needs it is incredibly wise." She felt Jeffrey pull back his hand and knew the answer. It was true. He was going to renege on his promise to them.

"Tamara, I don't know what to say."

She was tempted to respond, *Then don't say it. Go back and tell Eric that the kidney belongs to Mark—that he's the son who deserves it!* but she bit her tongue and waited him out.

"I went there this afternoon to speak to Eric—to tell him that I couldn't donate my kidney to him." Jeffrey put his hands over his face. "But I couldn't, Tamara, I couldn't do it."

She shook her head. "But you said that you thought everything through and you agreed that the right thing to do morally was to save the kidney for Mark, who may need it to survive in a few months time! Didn't you?" Her voice rose several notches at the end of the sentence.

"Yes, but—"

"Didn't you?" Tamara's face turned red with anger, and she repeated her question. "Didn't you tell us that?"

"I did," Jeffrey said solemnly. "Honestly, it's so hard to do this, believe me, it's—"

Tamara pushed her chair back and glared at him. "Yeah, so hard. But you don't have to do this. You can just keep your promise to Mark. To me. To your future grandchild."

Jeffrey slowly shook his head. "I wish I could, but I can't. There's no other way."

Tamara slammed her palm into the kitchen table. "You *wish*! What are you, a five-year old? You promised! Just the other day, you promised that you would save your kidney for Mark! What happened all of the sudden that you changed your mind? Do you want to kill Mark? You're doing that just with the psychological side of this roller coaster you're putting him through!"

Jeffrey slumped in his seat. "Eric's dying. Not in several months. Right now. I spoke with Ramsay, and the dialysis is barely keeping him alive." This time he looked her right in the eyes. "If they don't do the transplant within the next week, he'll die. I can't do that—I can't avoid responsibility and not try to save his life."

Tamara came back over to the table and grabbed Jeffrey's arm. "Just go. Get out! You sign Mark's death warrant by granting amnesty to a useless, hateful person—I just don't believe you can live with yourself!" She shouted. "Get the hell out of our apartment!"

Chapter Ten

Jeffrey pushed on into the biting wind as he turned the corner. After taking care of Vi, he'd paced back and forth in the little apartment, desperately seeking some kind of relief. But none was forthcoming. Punishment–that's what he needed; some form of penitence. So he left the artificial warmth of his building for the icy streets of downtown Bethesda. Initially the idea of penitence was calming–to feel the damp cold and suffer–but within fifteen minutes, he abandoned any attempt to expose himself to the chilly air and bundled up. Glancing at his watch, he saw that it was only 10:30 pm, way too early to get home. If he had a hope in hell of sleeping part of the night, he would need to come back to the apartment completely exhausted. Or drunk.

As he moved onto Elm Street, he saw the lit-up sign for The Barking Dog. He would have to take refuge from the cold for a while if he planned on staying out late. And he was thirsty. Not caring one way or another what kind of joint he went into, he opened the door and found a spot at the bar. He realized that this was the first time he had ever sat in a bar on a bar stool, and not at an actual table. He looked down at his hands. *Next thing you know I'll be telling the bartender all my troubles.*

He looked around the dim room filled with giant flat-screen TVs, each featuring a different sport: The Capitals, The Wizards–he could no longer keep track. As he half-heartedly scanned the room, hoping that no one he knew would be there, he noticed that everyone seemed happy. Or at least engaged in conversation, sports, or whatever. *Everyone but me.*

The bartender wiped the bar area clean and slid a bowl of mixed nuts over in Jeffrey's direction. He was young, but had a significant beer belly protruding over his belt, as though to demonstrate the benefits of drinking large quantities of draft beer. "Be right with you," he called to Jeffrey, and disappeared into the back.

Jeffrey was not hungry, but nibbled on a few salted nuts. When the bartender, whose tag said *Jack*, came back, he said, "What'll it be?"

Jeffrey wanted to blur his misery, but from experience he knew that he didn't have the physique to take in the three-plus beers that would be needed if he had any hope of numbing his pain. At the same time, he had essentially no experience with any hard liquor, with the exception of an unfinished "finger" of single malt whiskey when he and Annie had traveled to Scotland twenty years ago.

"How about a triple-shot of whiskey?"

Jack the bartender sighed. "We've got Kentucky Bourbon, Jim Beam, a variety of Irish blended and Scotch single malts–"

Jeffrey's eyes started to close–he put up his hands in mock defense. "Just… just give me a Scotch single malt–whatever you suggest. And get a second one ready."

Jack eyed him carefully. "You drive here?"

Jeffrey shook his head. "I live here in Bethesda. Well within walking distance. But if I look shaky when I'm done, please call me a cab."

Jack nodded in understanding and disappeared behind the bar to prepare the drink. Shoveling a couple handfuls of nuts into his mouth, Jeffrey glanced up to find a woman perched on the bar stool next to him. She had light brown hair with blond highlights, and Jeffrey guessed that she was in her mid forties–perhaps even close to fifty–but with her trim figure he couldn't be sure. She waved Jack over, ordered a glass of Chardonnay and turned to Jeffrey. "So you're new here."

As it wasn't really a question, more of a statement, and Jeffrey was struggling to hide the fact that he felt as though his sip of whiskey was burning a hole through his esophagus, he merely nodded. But then curiosity got the better of him. "Is it that obvious?"

She laughed easily. "Well, yeah. This place has its share of random visitors, and of course the sports crowds." She pointed at groups of mostly men huddled around the flat screens. "But most days it's the regulars, and you aren't one of them."

"And you are?"

She smiled, her pearly white teeth framing an attractive face. "Since I kicked out that son-of-a-bitch, yeah. It's lonely in my apartment."

Jeffrey had always heard stories about brazen women who looked to pick up strange men in bars, but never knew whether they were true or were more likely espoused as some fantasy by males in their mid-life crisis who took testosterone capsules in the hope of increasing their virility and the ratio of head to chest hair. It was two years since Annie died, and despite some gentle prodding from Mark and Tamara, he had not been able to think about the possibility of going out with a woman other than Annie.

"My name's Nina," said the woman, holding out her hand.

"Hi, I'm Jeffrey."

Did he imagine it, or was there a lingering squeeze before she dropped his hand? Not sure if he was excited or revolted by the thought of being picked up in a bar, he turned back to his drink.

"It sure is cold out," Nina said suddenly, turning toward Jeffrey. "I hear we could get some snow this weekend."

Swiveling forty-five degrees on his bar stool, Jeffrey considered this. He didn't want to hurt the woman's feelings, but he was in no mood to discuss the weather right now. "Uh, listen, Nina," he said, sounding awkward and patronizing even to his own ears. "I'm bad news right now—personal health problems in the family, and I'm having a hard time thinking about anything else." He grimaced, punctuating his troubles. "I don't normally drink, except for a little wine or beer, so I'm definitely out of my element here."

Jeffrey was rather surprised to find that Nina did not comment immediately. She waited perhaps a full minute, looking at him intently with a sympathetic expression, and tugged her purse open. Then she said, "It was nice meeting you, Jeffrey. I'm sorry about the circumstances. Perhaps we'll meet again under less stressful conditions." She handed him a card, dropped a ten-dollar bill on the bar, grabbed her jacket and headed for the door.

Surprised and not knowing if he had insulted her or if she really had sensed his tragic mood, he picked up her card. *Dr. Nina Kaufman, Chief, Adult Psychiatry Branch, National Institutes of Health.* Pocketing it, he raised his glass to his lips, swallowed, and as the burning sensation slid down his throat, waved to Jack for another round.

Chapter Eleven

Tamara poured herself another cup of coffee and dropped down hard on a chair at the kitchen table. She could feel the baby kicking; little butterfly wings fluttering inside. She knew that the extra stress was not a good thing for a pregnancy, but it was hard to stay calm. More than anything, it was Mark's unnatural calm; his willingness to just accept his father's idiotic decisions, that drove her crazy. How could he just give up like that? Why didn't he put pressure on his father; make him feel guilty like he should? Sometimes, she felt like kicking Mark in the butt. His passiveness was so goddamn annoying.

What to do? She could just sit here in the nice warm kitchen and wait until her shift began later in the afternoon. She was tempted to call Jeffrey, but decided there was no point. He wasn't going to budge. The only one who might be able to have an impact on him was Mark, and apparently that wasn't going to happen. No, she had to find some other way to get Jeffrey to save his kidney for Mark, and not waste it on that loser brother of his.

How could she force Jeffrey to change his mind? No, perhaps that was the wrong question. She had already tried to get him to change his mind, and that hadn't worked. So under what circumstances would Jeffrey save his kidney for Mark? In a flash, she knew the answer.

Tamara could have driven, but elected to travel by Metro so that she could think things out without worrying about the traffic. She had everything she needed, but she still had her reservations, despite her conviction that it had to be done. For Mark's sake. For her sake. And for the sake of the baby.

Even the off-peak hours on the Metro were not exactly quiet, but at least she found a seat. The young woman beside her was so wrapped up in her ear buds, that Tamara felt like she was alone. She slid her hand along the outer pouch of her handbag, not feeling the bulge initially, and her heart began hammering. But she soon realized that she was pressing on the wrong outer compartment, and rectifying her error, she confirmed that it was there. Relieved, she leaned back, and closed her eyes momentarily. Suddenly, the relief disappeared and was again replaced with the renewed wild beating of her heart and a suffocating feeling—like peanut butter stuck in her throat. She had never had that feeling before, but from her work at the hospital, particularly with parents of sick kids, she recognized it immediately: panic.

All morning, she'd wrestled with thoughts of whether she could do this. She knew that good and bad were not something that could be decided by the legal system. That was only a guideline put in place to look out for society in general: don't murder, steal, write fraudulent checks, and so on. But it wasn't designed as a philosophical template that could direct people through the gray areas of life. No such thing existed. It was up to her to take action and do the best she could. The ball was in her court, and she had to be proactive. This was what she had decided.

Jeffrey groaned, rolled over and swatted at his nightstand in a vain attempt to silence the annoying rendition of Beethoven's Fifth resounding from his phone. Before he could get his bearings and figure out that the loud banging noise in parallel to the music was not construction in his building, but indeed emanating from his own woozy head, a warm, wet sensation covered his face from ear to ear. Resigning himself to the onslaught and his hangover, Jeffrey lay back as Vi sprawled over his chest and licked his face diligently and methodically.

Taking his punishment without complaining, and realizing that it was Saturday morning and he had no immediate work-related responsibilities, he struggled to piece together the events of the previous evening. The drinks, a woman named Nina—no, a psychiatrist—did he dream that? Wait, she'd given him her card…

Climbing out of bed despite the combined protests of Vi and his aching head, he located his pants in the bathroom and found it in the back pocket. So he really had met a prominent NIH psychiatrist at the bar. And he had thought she was just some woman looking for a pickup. Well, wasn't she? She said that she was divorced. Wasn't that a straightforward attempt to hook up with the other sex? Then why was he embarrassed? Shouldn't she have been the embarrassed one? Maybe it didn't work that way; she might always be in her analysis mode. The shrink mode.

Not sure what to do, Jeffrey limped into the kitchen, replaced Vi's water, and fed her. Struggling into a pair of shoes, and wrapping a jacket around him, he ambled down the stairs and took her for her morning business. His mind was a blank; what the hell was he supposed to do? He knew that although Mark might somehow understand—or at least accept his decision—Tamara never would. She would forbid any contact with him, a traitor and enemy. By saving Eric with his kidney, Jeffrey was not only gambling with Mark's life, but with his future relationship with Mark and his family. In the best case scenario, Mark would soon find a perfect kidney match, undergo a transplant, and live happily with Tamara and their as-yet-unborn child for many years to come. But they would never forgive Jeffrey, and he would most likely never be a welcome part of that family.

At the same time, he wasn't naïve; once Eric had received his kidney and recovered, he would disappear again into his lowly underworld, full of scum and gangbangers. Leaving Jeffrey alone. He would be without his wife, without his two sons, without his future grandchild. So why was he choosing this route? He loved Mark, but didn't even like Eric. But he was a father to both sons, and blood was blood. Could he allow certain death of a son, albeit an unlikeable son, and gamble that the son he loved would survive without his kidney? What a decision! Even as these thoughts ran through his head, he knew that however angry he was at Eric, however bad Eric had been, he could not just sit by and watch him die. As the bile rose in his esophagus, he knew that he could not alter his decision.

Tamara arrived at the ward and immediately circled back to the elevators and over to the entrance lobby. She wiped the trickle of sweat off her forehead, and could feel another trickle of cool sweat along her spine. Being used to hospitals did not make this any easier. Gazing at some of the direction signs without seeing them, she focused hard on Mark, and his kidney disease. The fact that he would die without a successful transplant. And the idea that his worthless brother was several floors above her, biding his time on dialysis until her father-in-law donated his only spare kidney to him.

Mark was going to be a professor of biochemistry, a productive member of society–and a loving husband and father. What would Eric be? In and out of jail for the rest of his life? If Jeffrey didn't get it, if he couldn't read the writing on the wall–well, she could. And Tamara was an action person, not one of those talk-it-up people who were constantly throwing around cheap ideas and pseudo-philosophical thoughts. There were solutions for most problems, and even for those issues where there were no perfect solutions, one had to make the best of it. But not leave anything to chance when it was possible to improve the situation.

Feeling more confident after her internal pep talk, Tamara headed up the elevator again, getting off on the floor of the dialysis unit. Wrapping the new scarf that she had bought on the way tightly around her neck, and lowering her new baseball cap over her wig to shield her eyes, she straddled past the nurse station without raising any suspicions. Although Tamara worked in pediatric oncology, where security was enhanced due to the presence of children, she knew that all hospitals had CCTV cameras posted at key positions on each floor. She easily spotted the ones here, and made sure to look down, just in case. But this was all precaution, as she was certain that no one would ever suspect anything. It was just better to do things carefully.

Slowly, she wandered into the dialysis unit. An older man was just leaving the room, shuffling his feet along as he held onto a mobile saline dispenser. Scanning the room quickly, Tamara saw just one man in a reclining chair hooked up to a dialysis unit–Eric. She reached into her pocket and squeezed the syringe. Just to make sure she hadn't dropped it on the Metro. That would have been a disaster. She felt the tip of the syringe, with the capped needle at the end. The syringe held Fludrocortisone, a drug commonly used to increase blood pressure for those children in her ward with hypotension–low blood pressure. Of course, from talking with

Jeffrey, she knew that Eric's blood pressure was dangerously high, and that was the prime reason that the doctors were so anxious to do the transplant as soon as possible. Tamara also knew that the dose of Fludrocortisone that she intended to administer to his IV would spike his blood pressure to impossibly high levels and end his life quickly, and, she hoped, relatively painlessly. She was not a monster, after all, and hated to see suffering.

She could tell that Eric was dozing, an iPad lolling on his stomach. The resemblance to Mark was obvious, but he looked ten years older, with creased skin and a yellowish hue to his face. She sat in a chair beside him, all the while making calculations. His blood pressure and heart rate were monitored, and a sudden change would alert the duty nurse at the station. However, it would easily take 10-15 minutes before the Fludrocortisone that she injected would start to have any impact. By then, she would be at Metro Center, underground and miles from here. And no one would think to look for Fludrocortisone in the bloodstream of someone who already had dangerously high blood pressure. And even if they did, so what? They certainly wouldn't suspect his own family; most likely some poor over-worked nurse would get blamed for mixing up the meds. It happened all the time. Nurses were sleep deprived and under tremendous pressure. It really did happen all the time.

Just as Tamara was feeling inside her jacket pocket to remove the needle cap, a nurse waltzed in. She glanced briefly at Tamara, smiled, had a quick peek at Eric's monitors, and dodged back out of the room. Tamara knew that this was her chance—no one would be in over the next 15-20 minutes, and there was no way this busy nurse would ever remember what she looked like, blond wig and all, if she even remembered later that Eric had had a visitor. Popping the cap, she slowly pulled the syringe out of her jacket and bent over the IV drip.

Eric moved his hand, and she drew back and waited. Still asleep. But now, she hesitated. Eric, in sleep, looked peaceful; despite the severity of his condition, she could still see the stark resemblance to Mark. What had Mark told her about that one Hannukah... *"Mom and Dad bought us matching bicycles, but for some reason dad wrote my name on the card that went with each present. Eric started to cry. It was an honest mistake, but it was a typical reaction to Dad's... I don't know... to what Eric perceived as Dad's favoritism. Since Eric already*

88

thought Mom and Dad loved me more, it was just one more thing, I guess." She thought about the baby inside her, who she assumed would one day have a younger sibling. What if one felt unloved? What if she made some mistakes and one was left feeling like only the other one mattered? What a horrible thing that would be!

Tamara looked down at this man who was so foreign to her–about whom she had heard so much–most of it not very flattering. She saw his yellow, hollowed out face, and thought that this might be what Mark will look like, as an old man. If he gets to be an old man.

She gripped the syringe harder, and then a thought came to her. Eric would be her baby's uncle–Uncle Eric! And she would be the baby's mother–a mother who had murdered her brother-in-law. What kind of mother would she be? Would she ever be able to look her child in the eye and tell him–or her–to be a good person? To tell the truth? When she was about to take a life? It was murder, after all–even if Mark deserved to live while Eric did not. And how would she continue her relationship with Mark, knowing that she had killed his twin?

Sudden nausea swept through her. She could not do this. As much as she loved Mark and despised this imposter twin who was about to steal the greatest gift a father could bestow to his children, she still could not take his life. She was failing Mark, and she wasn't used to failing at anything. But as a nurse, she could never purposefully end someone's life. Capping the needle in her pocket and with tears of anguish sliding down her cheeks, she hurried into the ladies' room and shut herself into a stall. *What have I become? What was I even thinking?*

As she squeezed the Fludrocortisone out of the syringe into the toilet and flushed, she knew she was also flushing away her dreams of saving Mark.

Still queasy, Jeffrey shuffled papers around his desk, trying to justify his decision to come into work on a Saturday morning. He often spent long hours on weekends poring over his computer, answering emails from colleagues and postdocs in his own lab, but he seldom went in to the office. It was more comfortable working with a laptop from his recliner, shoes off and feet up–although admittedly he was somewhat less productive with Vi on his lap.

This morning, however, despite his severe hangover, Jeffrey was in his office. He was having trouble admitting to himself why he had come in to work, and was trying to rationalize his behavior by writing it off as a necessity to advance Jai's manuscript. But having just returned a newly-edited version to Jai a day earlier, he knew that he was fooling himself; there was no way that Jai would have read it and made the corrections that he requested before the weekend was over. No, that was not why he had come to the NIH this morning.

With a sigh, Jeffrey took his wallet from his backpack and left the backpack behind his desk. He put on his jacket, and found himself moving inexorably toward the mother of all brick buildings–Building 10. Entering through the cafeteria, he looked again at Nina's card. Her office was on the ninth floor, and he took the busy elevators up, stopping on every floor along the way so people could exit or get on.

He wiped sweat from his brow. Hungover still? Maybe. He felt dizzy, too, and weirdly like he was functioning from outside his body; like watching himself on a TV show.

When he finally arrived on the ninth floor, he avoided making eye contact with anyone, and it made him think of his twins, years ago, childishly thinking that if they couldn't see you, you couldn't see them. In the men's room he washed his face, then stared at himself in the mirror for what felt like a long time. What the hell was he doing here? It was Saturday! Nina–Dr. Nina Kaufman–wasn't going to be here on a Saturday. And even if she was, what was he going to do, march in and say, "My name is Jeffrey Coleman, and I have a problem?"

He took a deep breath, let it out slowly, and left the men's room, walking down the hallway until he saw the sign that said *Adult Psychiatry Branch*. When he tried the door, it was unlocked, and a young African American woman looked up from her seat at the desk. "Can I help you?"

Startled, Jeffrey replied "Uh, no, I mean, I, uh–"

"This is a private office, so if you have no business here, I'll have to ask you to leave, please."

Jeffrey took a step forward, summoning up his dignity. "I'm Dr. Coleman. Chief of the Biochemistry and Molecular Cell Biology

Branch here at NIBBR–the National Institute for Basic Biomedical Research. I'd like to see Dr. Kaufman, if she's in."

There was a marked straightening of the administrator's spine, and she answered, "I'm sorry Dr. Coleman, but Dr. Kaufman has clinical consultations all morning. May I leave her a message?"

Jeffrey smiled weakly. "Sure." Not having a fancy business card, he wrote his name, email address and cell phone number on a slip of paper, and handed it to the woman. "It would be great if she could give me a call."

Waiting in front of the elevators, wondering whether Dr. Kaufman would even remember him, let alone call, he heard a voice say, "Jeffrey?"

And there she was, dressed in a white lab coat, striding toward him. "Thank goodness for these slow elevators," she said. "I wanted to catch you in person."

Surprised and too confused to think of anything meaningful to say, Jeffrey blurted out, "I thought you had consultations all morning?" Immediately, he regretted the defensiveness in his voice.

"I do," Nina answered. "But I am allowed the occasional bathroom break." She smiled, and then turned serious. "Are you okay? How about lunch here, at the cafeteria?"

Jeffrey also smiled, but it was not a whole-hearted smile, and its inherent sadness radiated from his face. "Yes, that would be great. Thanks." He stepped onto the elevator that had finally arrived, and waved awkwardly. "See you at noon."

Returning to his office, Jeffrey brushed his teeth and changed into a clean shirt that he saved in his filing cabinet for occasions that required better attire. Still over an hour to go, he thought, glancing again at his watch. He tried calling Eric at the hospital, but there was no answer. He hoped that didn't mean there had been a further deterioration. At least that's what he hoped that he hoped– but if Eric died, he wouldn't need... *Stop, don't think about it.*

Walking over to the lab, Jeffrey found several of his post-doctoral fellows busy at work. He nodded and smiled, aware that it was no longer a simple or trivial thing for him to do, and finally found Jai over at his desk. "Ah, Jeffrey. I didn't know you were in. I was about to write you an email."

Jeffrey waved his hand nervously. "Don't. Erase it, right away." He looked around the lab, but everyone was busy either doing

91

experiments at the bench, or plugging away on their own computers and laptops. "Nothing should be in writing, Jai. No emails to your brother or me or to anyone else."

Jai was surprised. "Why?"

Jeffrey glanced at his watch. "Come with me to my office—I have less than an hour, but we need to talk."

On the short walk over, Jeffrey told Jai that government emails—in fact any emails—were not safe. Anything unethical that they were planning to do had to be done by in person conversations—or at the worst, by phone.

"The best way is by burner-phones—you know, the pre-paid ones that you can get at Best Buy or any electronic store. And we need to pay with cash, so our credit cards can't be traced."

Jai looked at him in amazement. "Jeffrey, first of all, I was going to let you know this morning that everything has already been done—and it's okay, all by phone with Alok, no emails."

"But with your *own* cell phone?" Jeffrey pressed.

Jai raised his eyebrows. "Of course, Jeffrey. Why wouldn't I talk to my own brother with my own phone? There's nothing inherently criminal about that."

Jeffrey sighed. "I suppose you're right. I'm just not used to this kind of thing."

They were now in Jeffrey's office, with the door closed, although there was no one around in the administrative suite on weekends. Jai leaned forward and clasped his hands. "It's done Jeffrey." He pulled a flash drive from his pocket linked to a key ring. "I've got it right here. There was a ton of files, most of it not relevant to our plan, so I disposed of everything else." He winked at Jeffrey. "Including the entire PI report that Danfield solicited from a detective to follow his wife around. Nasty divorce, alimony, that kind of thing." He raised is hands in a hands-off gesture. "Not my business."

Jeffrey rolled his eyes uncomfortably. "Let's stick to our business, Jai." He glanced at his watch. "I don't have a lot of time."

Jai handed him the flash drive, and they opened Danfield's file on the project on Jeffrey's personal laptop—one that he had bought on his own dime, so it wasn't deemed a government computer.

They went through the data several times, with Jeffrey taking some notes on a legal pad—so that he would have the proper ammunition ready when he confronted Danfield on the phone. When they were done and Jeffrey had what he needed, he said, "Can Alok destroy the louse now?"

"Absolutely," said Jai. "All he has to do is go back in through the garage door and use the nit-remover-shampoo that he designed. No one will ever know."

"Then go ahead," Jeffrey said. "And only by phone. Even though I can't imagine that anyone would ever know what you are talking about with this nit-remover-shampoo."

"Of course," said Jai. "Will do."

When Jai had left his office, Jeffrey ignored the 46 new emails in his inbox, including second reminders that some of the manuscripts he was reviewing were overdue. He would wait for the third reminders. In his experience, reviewing in *too* timely a manner often had the effect of creating more requests for reviews. Exiting email, he went to Google and learned that Dr. Nina Kaufman was one of those rare birds who held both a medical doctor or MD, as well as a doctor of philosophy, or Ph.D. degree, and that she had graduated from Washington University in St. Louis. He could see from the NIH's free archive of biomedical research journals that she was a prolific researcher with almost 200 publications in her name. But could it really be the same Nina Kaufman who'd also been a professional tennis player? Impressive.

At the cafeteria, she came right up to him, held out her hand, and smiled. "Nice to formally meet you, Dr. Coleman."

"You, too," he managed to say. "Please call me Jeffrey."

They both filled their plates at the salad bar, and found a table. "I wanted to apologize for being rude to you last night," Jeffrey said as soon as they sat. "I'm not normally like that." He paused, almost hoping that Nina would cut him off, and perhaps tell him that he hadn't really been rude. That it was okay. But she didn't. So he prattled on, feeling himself dig a bigger hole as he continued. "I just had a rough day. Or more accurately, a rough week." He stopped again, but Nina was just staring at him with an almost expressionless gaze. "Well, I guess it didn't help that I was drinking. I, er, don't usually have much more than a glass of wine. Or a beer."

When he stopped to fork up a bite of salad, Nina finally spoke. "I don't usually go over and talk to strange men in bars. But you

93

looked familiar. I thought I had seen you here at the NIH. And you looked *so* out of place in that bar." She also started on her salad.

"Yes, I was definitely out of my element in there. I don't get out much since… "

Casually, Nina asked "Since?"

In spite of himself, Jeffrey forced a little smile. "You're not going to send me a bill for this consultation?"

Nina smiled. "Even as a Branch Chief, I'm not sure you'd be able to afford me. But I hope your joke wasn't a ploy to change the subject?"

Jeffrey's feeble smiled withered. "Since my wife Annie died, about two years ago."

Nina nodded in understanding. "But," she pointed at him with her fork, "that's obviously not why you were in the bar last night; out of your element, as you say."

Jeffrey looked everywhere but at Nina. As the silence ensued, he finally turned back to her. "You know, when Annie was sick and then… died… " he paused for a deep breath, "I didn't think things in my life could possibly get any worse. But I was wrong."

Her warm eyes encouraged him to go on, and so he did— explaining the current situation, and then going back twenty years to tell her of the twins' childhood and Eric's alienation. Nina asked the occasional clarifying question, but mostly just listened, with a placid expression on her face. When Jeffrey was done, he pushed his chair back slightly, stretched his legs out, and took a protracted gulp of water. "I feel so tired, like I could climb into bed and sleep for a week."

Nina nodded. "When something is weighing heavily on your mind and you finally unburden yourself, that's what it feels like. It's a good thing. Have you told anyone else, or have you been keeping it all inside?"

"Just Mark and his wife. Mark and I have always been close."

Nina shook her head. "It's good that you're close, but he's definitely not what you'd call an impartial observer. You're bearing the entire weight of this… this horrible task of making a decision. And someone is going to be the loser. Whichever way you turn, whatever you decide, there will always be guilt." She pursed her lips. "That's about as hard as it gets. No wonder you were in The Barking Dog."

Feeling weary and suddenly wanting to change the subject, he said, "And you? You did mention something about a divorce? Were you also trying to forget something in The Barking Dog? Or didn't you say you were a 'regular?'"

"Yeah," Nina exhaled. "A regular. Just so you know I'm not an alcoholic. By 'regular' I meant once a month. Last Friday of every month."

Jeffrey looked puzzled, and was torn between wanting to find out more and being careful not to pry into Nina's personal business. But curiosity won over–and after all, he had just finished telling this woman his life story. "I would never have mistaken you for an alcoholic. It was me who barely remembers getting home last night." He paused, and then: "So why do you go every month?"

"Well, I guess I can honestly say it's not for the quality of the wine," she laughed, "It's a long story–are you sure you want to hear it?"

"Of course," he said. "Why wouldn't I?"

"Well, it's been my experience that not everyone likes to listen. And being a professional listener myself, I wouldn't want to impose on you."

"I would much rather listen than talk," Jeffrey said. "What I told you these last thirty minutes was so uncharacteristic of me–almost like me being in The Barking Dog."

"I guess I'm just reluctant to spill the beans. My story highlights the weak points in my life, and I don't typically look for opportunities to do that."

"I won't hold it against you, I promise."

"Well, since you promise." Nina leaned forward, elbows on the table, and folding her hands together, she used the bridge to prop up her chin. "Several years ago, my marriage began to unravel. William is a software engineer, and he always traveled a lot from work, but he began spending more and more time away from home. One time, our older son David was really sick. He had a high fever and pain in his lower abdomen. The right side. It was late, like 11:00 pm, but having gone through medical school all those years ago I couldn't help suspect that it was appendicitis–so I took him to the ER."

Jeffrey nodded. He'd had his own appendix removed as a young adult, and it had been a very painful experience. But he remained silent.

"So I tried calling William on his cell and he wasn't answering. He was supposed to be in Denver, so it was only 9:00 pm there, but there was no answer." She took a sip of her iced tea and continued. "I called William's boss Rich. He wasn't really a boss-boss, but more like the guy who coordinated the projects for the engineers in the company. Anyway, Rich told me that William didn't have any work-related project in Denver, and that he hadn't actually had any company travel for several months."

Jeffrey frowned, knowing what was coming.

"As you can imagine," Nina said, "He was having an affair. With a 26-year old law student, right here in DC. Of course, after the fact, it seemed logical. He was cold, uninterested, as though his mind was always somewhere else, for months before that. But here I was, with a kid going into surgery, and his father had checked out and was busy bonking someone 23 years younger." She shrugged. "Well that was the beginning of our long, drawn-out and messy divorce."

Waiting a few seconds, Jeffrey asked, "And how old was David?"

"Fifteen. And Mel–Melody–was just nine. It was rough for them."

"And you."

"Well I got through the day-to-day routine pretty well, for the most part. But I was so wrapped up in dealing with my own issues that I... " She stopped, and to his surprise, wiped away sudden tears. "I... I may have miscalculated with a depressed patient. I didn't catch the urgency of it in time. He... he committed suicide." She sighed. "And that's why I go to The Barking Dog.

"Nina," Jeffrey said gently, "you can't... I mean, depressed people commit suicide all the time. Psychiatry may be an effective tool, but it's not an exact science! How can you possibly fault yourself?"

"Rationally I know that I can't foresee everything, and that psychiatry isn't an exact science. I'm not even sure it's really a science at all. But when the family sued and the American Medical

Association began an inquiry, it shook my confidence. Even if the AMA found the complaint against me groundless."

"Well there you go."

"Such a tragedy for the family. But you're right, it's impossible to account for everything, and every practicing psychiatrist I know has had cases like this."

"I can imagine."

"So," her turn to change the subject, "what's next for you? Are you going through with the kidney donation next week?"

"I don't have the luxury of waiting. Eric will die if he doesn't get a kidney right away."

"It's Saturday, so there's nothing you can do right now."

"No. Just brood and stew," he said, dreading the weekend ahead.

"Or... " she hesitated.

"Or... what?"

"Or we could both go back to work, and meet up again tonight. Get out. Would do us both a world of good, don't you think?"

He was surprised by her invitation, but at the same time, not surprised. "Yes," he said, "a world of good."

Chapter Twelve

Nina Kaufman smiled to herself and headed out to the car park behind Building 10 at the NIH. It had been over two years since she had been asked out by a guy–at least by a man who wasn't half-drunk and trying to hit on her at The Barking Dog. Well, technically, Jeffrey hadn't asked her out–she had asked him. But she knew that he had wanted to–he was just one of those shy guys who has trouble being the initiator. That was a problem she never had– she typically asked for what she wanted, and got it.

She put her car in drive and headed toward Old Georgetown and south in the direction of Bethesda, fighting traffic even on a Saturday afternoon. Parents were driving kids to activities, and everyone was shopping: groceries, DIY, furniture. There were so many people in the Beltway area, many of whom were temporary residents, and shopping was a common activity that clogged the area's streets and strip malls.

Nina hummed off key as she surfed channels on the radio. Her son David, who now a high school senior, had been trying to convince her to spend the time to set up a playlist or connect to– what was that application? Spotify. But she never seemed to have the time or patience to bother learning how to do it. "I'll do it for you, Mom, but you need to tell me what songs and artists you want." Ah, well, one day, she thought, and continued to hum that tune that had infiltrated her brain. She didn't even know what it was or where she had heard it, but it seemed to be caught like a stubborn piece of apple peel between her teeth.

Nina thought back to her conversation with Jeffrey; it had been ages since she had told her story about William's betrayal and the breakup of her marriage. Unlike many other women who had gone through a traumatic divorce, Nina was fully aware that she was not traumatized. She was neither melancholic nor bitter. She had felt tremendous anger at the time, and that anger had slowly turned to a more moderate form of resentment. And finally, when William's young law student threw him over for a partner in a law firm, she had pitied him. He had hinted and hemmed and hawed, but was ultimately too proud to beg Nina to take him back–not that she would have anyway, the bastard. But she lost the remainder of her anger and realized that he was simply weak; weaker than she had thought when she married him. And definitely weaker than her. He was ruled by the zipper in his pants–what did her granny always say? He couldn't keep it in his pants–that was it. Well, that lusty feeling was fine for a fling–maybe even a year or two at the beginning of a relationship. But if he valued her–and their relationship–less than a roll or two in the hay with a fresh spring chicken? Well, then he wasn't for her. Let him explain himself to the kids. And now, after these few years alone–was there a possibility of someone new on the horizon? She stopped humming and began to sing, pressing the car window fully closed so as not to offend the ears of any fellow drivers or pedestrians.

Nina left the car in her driveway, and climbed the four steps up to her front door. Like many homes in the area, it did not have a garage–her house was an older one, and none of the previous owners had built a stand-alone garage or carport. Before turning her key in the lock, she reflected on how they had planned on living there for only a short time–she and William. It was–what did they call it–a starter home. It was fine, of course, a nice neighborhood of brownstones, with mature trees–but the houses were relatively small. Hers had only three bedrooms and one and a half bathrooms. But with David soon to go off to college, and Mel just five years behind, it was almost too big. As she entered and heard the tumultuous racket echoing from David's drum set in the basement, she felt that perhaps she was mistaken; and wished the house was large enough to isolate the noise.

Knowing that there was no way on earth that he would hear her, she trudged down the stairs and waved. The thumping stopped momentarily, and David acknowledged her briefly, "Hi, Mom."

"Hi David, did you have some lunch?"

"No, I'll eat later. I have to finish practicing—the guys from the band are coming over this evening to jam."

Nina smiled. "Good thing I won't be home this evening."

"Hot date?" David smashed the cymbal theatrically.

Blushing slightly, Nina said, "Actually, yes." Once William had left them, he had had such a string of women to which he had introduced his children on their weekly visits that neither Abby nor David had any problem with their mother dating. If only she had had the time or inclination.

"Good for you. If he's good looking, make sure you get a photo together and I'll put it up on my Facebook page so that Dad can eat his heart out."

"Thanks, David, but you know I'm not trying to compete with him." She sighed. "I wasn't looking to meet anyone, but this was just a freak thing—he's a scientist—actually another branch chief at NIH."

"Cool!" David pounded the cymbal again, hard enough so that Nina worried about the fillings in her teeth. "As long as he's not a shrink like you."

Mark's eyes glazed over as he pondered the "legalese" on the screen. Why did those bloody lawyers have to make every sentence such a challenge to understand? For God's sake, he had a Ph.D.—twenty years of education, and he could barely understand the wording of the will he had just downloaded. Were they purposefully trying to confuse people? Or was it all a lawyer-like ploy to show the general population that they were needed in this internet age when people could already find ready-made contracts for just about everything?

He wasn't even sure that a will was necessary, assuming that all of his worldly possessions would automatically go to Tamara. He knew that the other two clauses that he wanted to include were not exactly standard-fare, but what the hell, it was *his* life—and death, after all. It was his right to stipulate whatever he wanted; his last opportunity to make himself heard. So he typed the following points: 1) to his father, that he loved him and wanted him to have the right to visit his grandchild even after Mark's death, and 2) that he bore no grudge or ill-will to Eric, and wished him a full recovery and a renewed relationship with dad. That was all. Did people put clauses like that in their wills? Mark didn't care; he wouldn't be around to hear the criticism anyway. He didn't know if there was anything he could possibly do to help make Tamara feel more generous to his father, and while he couldn't blame her, he couldn't blame his father, either. In fact, he couldn't blame anyone, not even Eric. His brother was far sicker than he was right now, suffering terribly, and all Mark wanted was for things to go back to the way they were. It would be better if Eric changed into a different, nicer person, but Mark would settle for everyone being healthy again. But that wasn't going to happen, unless a kidney donor suddenly appeared on the horizon.

Slogging through the verbiage, Mark added his own wording, and finally printed and signed the document, carefully placing it in an envelope. He would stop on the way home at his friend Allan's apartment—one of his few remaining high school buddies in the area—and get him to sign as a witness. There was no need for a notary or lawyer or any other official to be there. Enough was enough.

When he finally arrived home at 1:00 pm with his newly-signed and witnessed will firmly sealed in a manila envelope, he found Tamara lying on the couch and unresponsive to his greeting. It didn't take a husband and devoted partner to realize she was upset, but the magnitude of her stress had Mark very worried. It wasn't like her to lie down any time; she was always a human dynamo, constantly on the move. She reminded him of an electron from Heisenberg's principle of uncertainty—that one could never actually pin down where the electron was in any given point in time—it was only possible to provide a statistical probability of where that electron might actually be.

"Tamara? Can I sit down?"

No answer. She lay, staring fixedly at the ceiling, hands crossed over her chest. Mark sat on the floor near her head. "You know," he said gently, sliding his fingers to intertwine with hers, "you still have your whole life ahead of you. I mean," he corrected, "we both do. It's just that right now, your whole life looks a lot longer than mine."

She still did not look at him, but he saw that there were tears forming in the corner of her left eye, the one he could see from his side, and they were starting to stream down her cheeks.

Is this really happening? Jeffrey wondered as he strolled arm in arm with Nina through the dark streets of Bethesda. The most depressing, terrifying, tumultuous time of his life, and here he was, strongly attracted to a woman he'd just met. Steering her gently to his right, he tipped his head. "There it is, The Barking Dog. Where it all started."

"Where it all started," Nina repeated. "But it doesn't have to end there. Would you like to invite me back to your place? I'd invite you to mine, but it's a complete mess."

Jeffrey caught his breath. "Uh, well... I'd like to, but I'm afraid I might disappoint you. I'm just not sure I can, er, perform very well. With, well, the transplant next week and all that's going on. And... " He looked at her briefly before looking away again. "I haven't been with anyone since Annie... I don't know if I can... well, I don't know."

Nina didn't answer right away, and when she did, her voice was soothing. "I'm not trying to be pushy and force my own agenda, but I think you're mixing two separate things."

"What do you mean?"

"Your ability to... perform, as you say. We can be together and enjoy each other's company tonight without having to worry about outcomes. That's not an issue for me, and it's only an issue for you if you make it one." She paused as if to let him comment, and when he didn't, she went on, "The question is, are you ready to be gentle with yourself and treat yourself with honor."

"Treat myself with honor?

"Yes. Give yourself a break, Jeffrey. It's been two years since your wife died. You need to decide whether you want to continue to sink with the ship, or be a survivor. You could mourn for the rest of your life, immerse yourself in work, and wake up 20 years from now alone and with the realization that you will continue to be alone until you die. Some people do that when they lose a spouse." Again, she gave him a chance to respond, and again he didn't. "I don't think you're happy. It's up to you to decide how you want to live."

Jeffrey shook his head. "But it's not about me. What would Mark say? It would be hard enough to explain this without the transplant and everything else going on... "

"No, Jeffrey," Nina said quietly, "it *is* about you. Two years is a long time to wait before starting a new relationship–believe me, I deal with clients in mourning all the time."

"But... "

"It feels like less to you because you grieve every day, every single day without a break. But two years is a good long time. It's time you started living again."

"It's just that... starting a new relationship *now* seems so... trivial. And self-centered. Eric is dying, and Mark might... I mean I hope he won't, but he... "

"Jeffrey," Nina interrupted, "relationships–including sex and intimacy–are a central part of life. Not something that you ignore or put off because your life is troublesome. Relationships help us get through the rough patches."

She waited while he processed it; used to people not being able to think of themselves. Many of her clients had an easier time doing for others, perhaps in some ways they thought it was easier than dealing with their own issues.

"So," he said finally, "you don't think it's selfish for me to be pursuing my own pleasure when I have two sick sons, and I'm donating a kidney to one of them next week?"

"Not one bit. I know the risk is very small for you, but you are giving up a kidney. At least theoretically, it's a serious procedure. Are you not entitled to live out your life to the fullest right now? Sick kids or not?"

"Well, I don't know."

"Hey, aren't I the professional here?" she teased, because she realized the conversation was getting too intense for him. "Anyone else, I would have charged an arm and a leg for what I just told you."

He laughed. Their eyes met, and he felt the warmth in hers. "Maybe," he said.

"Besides," she said, sensing that it was okay to get serious again, "Annie would want you to be happy. Think about it."

He sighed. "Okay, I will."

Mark had told Tamara he'd come to bed later, but he knew he wouldn't; he knew he'd be awake all night, and didn't want to keep her up with his restlessness. As an expectant mother, she needed her sleep.

At 4:00 in the morning he gave up trying, turned on a lamp, and tried to read the novel he'd begun a month ago. But after reading the same paragraph three times without the words registering in his brain, all he could think was *When I started this book my life was so normal. My life was great. Everything about my life was great.* Already, he'd started dividing his life into Before the Diagnosis and After. Earlier in the year, he and Tamara had been driving home from the market, and another driver cut them off. Rage had filled him, absolutely filled every single cell, and he started gesturing and swearing. Looking back on his reaction, it seemed ridiculous.

If only Tamara wasn't angry with him. On top of what he was dealing with, he lacked the emotional endurance to break through her icy wall. *"You can't ask your father to do this, you have to tell him!"* she had shouted at him. Like it was so easy to bully his father into doing something he considered morally wrong. He loved his sons equally, no matter what the circumstances. That's what made him a good father. But that's what Eric could never understand or believe.

Mark shut out the light and lay on his back staring at the ceiling. On the other hand, Tamara's feelings were valid: Eric didn't deserve the kidney. He'd been the bad son, the mean son, the son who had barely made it to his mother's funeral, for Christ's sake.

Maybe I should talk to Dad. The thing is, it's not just for me—it's for my family. My child. His grandchild. That should count for more than just being fair.

Back and forth he went; emotions wrestling with logic, until the sun started peeking in the window, and at last he slept. When he awoke at 8:45, Tamara had already left for work.

"Are you alright?"

Jeffrey, lying with Nina in his arms, said, "I am. Why?"

"There's a disconnect between your answer and your body language."

He took a moment to work out his response, and came up with, "This was wonderful... but... it's just that, I feel like it's wrong to be happy or even satisfied right now. With my sons being ill... my daughter-in-law being upset."

Nina took his hand under the sheets. "You know, Jeffrey, as we age, every day there's a greater chance that something can go wrong with our bodies. That's just the way it is. And we see it happening to our friends and acquaintances, too." She rolled onto her side and faced him. "I think we have to be vigilant about carrying on with the good parts of life, even in the face of adversity. If we let every depressing thing get us down, we'd never be able to enjoy any part of our lives."

"Nina, we're not talking about people in their seventies and eighties. These are my two sons, both in their twenties."

"I know. It's not easy or simple. But you're doing everything that you possibly can, and more. You're donating a kidney, and yet you feel that you don't deserve to live your own life. Does that make sense?"

"None of this makes any sense."

"Jeffrey, ask yourself this question honestly: Would you not be feeling the same way about things even if neither of your sons were sick? Wouldn't you just be using Annie's death to say the same thing?"

"No," he answered promptly; defensively. But Nina did this for a living, and waited patiently while he reconsidered. "Okay, maybe. But that doesn't matter, because they *are* sick."

"No Jeffrey, that is the point. You have put your own life on hold, regardless of your sons, or anything else. It's *you* who has to decide: move forward or stay stuck."

Mark took the car because he knew he had to practice getting those words out in the right order, and with just the right tone—and there was no way that he could speak aloud on the Metro. As he made the drive out in the ever-awakening Sunday morning traffic of Wisconsin Avenue, he rehearsed over and over: *Dad, you know I don't want to interfere with your decision, and you know that I haven't criticized you since you made the choice of donating your kidney to Eric. But that's not the problem. It's Tamara. She'll never forgive you. Even if Eric lives, and I live and the baby is fine—she'll never let you be a part of the baby's life. You've got to think of her, and the baby, and yourself. You don't want to be left with just Eric. I don't need to forgive you, because I don't feel the way Tamara does—I understand what you're facing. But Tamara is almost like a daughter to you. Think of Tamara and yourself in this case, leave me out of it. And ask*

105

yourself, is it worth losing a daughter and grandchild? This is your real family. I'll respect whatever you decide, Dad, but you've got to think about all of the consequences.

Would it even make a dent in his father's thought processes? Mark didn't know. But at this point, that's all he had left to try. So he continued to go over and over his spiel, even as he drove into Bethesda and began searching for a parking place near his father's apartment.

Not wanting to cause Vi to start barking, Mark avoided knocking on the door, and quietly let himself in with his key. In between great leaps of happiness, in which Vi's springy jumps propelled her into Mark's line of forward vision, Mark became aware of someone sitting at the kitchen table. In a bathrobe. His mother's bathrobe, to be precise; the bathrobe so favored by his mother that his father had not been able to include it in the articles slated for Goodwill.

"What the hell?" he blurted.

The woman in his mother's robe stood. She was lovely; tall and elegant. "You must be Mark."

"And who the hell are you?"

"Nina Kaufmann–a new friend of your father's. Nice to meet you. I've heard so much about–"

"My dad is having a kidney removed next week," Mark interrupted. "What are you doing here? What's going on?"

"Mark," said Jeffrey. "Hi."

"Dad, what are you doing with this bimbo? What's the matter with you?"

Nina watched Jeffrey's eyes widen, and she wondered how he would react. But she remained silent, knowing that this conversation was not about her.

Jeffrey walked up to Mark, and putting a hand on his shoulder, said, "Sit down, let's talk."

Mark jerked away. "I can't believe you, Dad! First you decide to give Eric your kidney, and then I come home and this woman is sitting at the table in Mom's bathrobe! How can you do that? It's disrespectful! It's an insult to Mom's memory!"

"Mark, Nina is a close friend. We met a few days ago, and… "

"A few days ago? Close friend, my ass! What kind of close friend would do something like this, with everything going on in your life right now? This makes me so sick."

"Mark, calm down. Nina is the Chief of the Adult Psychiatry—"

"I don't give a shit *who* she is!"

"Mark, you need to listen to me." Jeffrey pulled out a chair. "Please sit down."

"Thanks but no thanks! It's one thing to screw me over and give a kidney to the son who couldn't care less if you're even alive, but it's another thing to screw around on Mom!"

Jeff drew in a deep breath. "Mark, I won't have you talk to me that way. And I won't have you insult my friend."

Mark turned around, and without looking back, slammed the door and headed down the stairs.

Chapter Thirteen

Tamara stirred the lentil soup boiling gently on the range, and then sat down wearily at the kitchen table. Despite her long shift on the ward, she was determined to prepare some home-cooked food for Mark. She had noticed that he was not eating very much recently; picking at his food without interest, and his clothes were hanging on him.

Hearing footsteps on the porch, she glanced at the clock: not even five–he was early! She rose and hurried into the hallway to greet him. There was fumbling with the lock, an uncharacteristic muttered string of profanities, and then at last he swung open the door and stumbled in. Tamara gaped at him: shirt untucked and halfway unbuttoned, swaying and reeking of beer.

"Mark! What's going on?"

"Wha, whooses anythin' gonnon?"

"You're drunk!" Tamara couldn't have been more surprised if he'd come in wearing a prom gown. "What's the matter with you? You're supposed to be looking for a faculty position!"

"M'fine."

"Really smart, to go out drinking! It's irresponsible and dangerous! With your kidney problems... " She looked at him warily. "Is that what you want? To die before you can even get a transplant and leave me alone with a new baby? The coward's way out?"

"No, no. It's juss... I can't truss anyone right now. My own father... hooking up with some bimbo. In Mom's bathrobe! Christ."

"What are you talking about?"

"Need t'pee."

She watched him stumble to the bathroom. Bimbo? That didn't sound much like the Jeffrey she knew. Was Mark having some kind of psychotic breakdown?

When he returned, he sat at the kitchen table and put his head down and moaned.

"What are you talking about, Mark? What bimbo?" she asked again.

"Wen to his apar'ment–she was in thuh kitchen."

Sitting across from him she said, "Who, Mark? Who was in the kitchen?"

Mark looked up, confused. "Jus' us in kitchen, Tamara."

Tamara lost her patience. "Mark! Who was in *your dad's* kitchen?"

"Uh. She said her name. Nina. Yeah, Nina." He plopped his head back on the table.

"And she was in your dad's apartment wearing a bathrobe?"

"*Mom's* bathrobe. Red terrycloth."

"And your dad didn't say what she was doing there?"

"Dunno."

"Mark. Answer me!"

"Her name was Nina. Thas' all I know."

Leaving him at the kitchen table, Tamara went into the bedroom and tried to calm herself. After half an hour she heard chair slide away from the table, and then she heard Mark's heavy footfalls. Hoping he wouldn't come in, she was relieved to hear him flop on the couch. Probably the trip down the hall would have been too much. Immediately she heard his spastic snores, interrupted occasionally by a dry, rasping noise from his throat.

With her hands clasped across her belly, she still needed to come up with a plan. And right away, she did: If it was true, if Jeffrey was sleeping with some bimbo as Mark said, then the last thing he'd want would be for anyone to find out. Blackmail? She sighed. How shameful, to do this to him when his life was already so difficult. But they were running out of time: the double surgery was in three days.

But what if... what if Mark got the story wrong because he was drunk? Tamara couldn't imagine Jeffrey entertaining a bimbo; and not just entertaining–if she was sitting at the table in a bathrobe, it meant she'd probably spent the night. Jeffrey, with his shy ways, and his reluctance to find a new girlfriend after Annie died… it didn't make sense.

But it was all Tamara had. She needed to stake out his apartment and wait. Get pictures, get the bimbo's name. Then threaten to blow the whistle if he didn't change his mind about giving Mark his kidney.

Even before she pulled up and shut off the engine she wondered if she was doing the right thing. Maybe she could just go up to his door and knock, and then take a picture. No, best to get photos and then approach him. That would show him that she was serious.

So she sat and waited, nibbling on some dry fruit. She was thirsty, but hadn't brought water, fearing her bladder would fill before Jeffrey appeared with Nina. Not only that, but every fifteen minutes the car started to feel like an industrial refrigerator, and she had to keep turning on the engine. Afraid of getting carbon monoxide poisoning, she needed to open the window until she cut the engine again. And every single time she started the engine, a driver would suddenly appear behind her and spot her exhaust, put on his signal, assuming she was pulling out, and wait patiently. Then he would become angry as he realized minutes later that she had no intention of pulling out.

Just after 7:00 pm, as she was thinking about going home, the door to Jeffrey's apartment building opened, and out came a tall, slender woman wearing a ski hat, followed by Jeffrey. Grabbing her Pentax with a 200 mm telephoto lens, Tamara quickly took half a dozen photos while the pair was still illuminated at the entrance to the apartment building. Jeffrey holding the door, Jeffrey taking her arm, the two walking with arms around each other's waist. *Disgusting. His son might be dying of an untreatable kidney disease, and he's not only going to do nothing to save him; he's bopping this fly-by-night bimbo! She's probably trying to get him to change his will so that my child and I get nothing!*

Fueled by rage, Tamara snapped at least forty photos before her father-in-law and his company disappeared from sight in the direction of Wisconsin Ave.

When she got home, Mark was still asleep on the couch. Compassion tugged at her heart. She was angry with him for getting drunk, but she felt sorry for him, too. The sight of him, so vulnerable… his steady breathing, the faint whistling noise as he exhaled air through his front teeth… Gently, she covered him with a blanket, and went to bed.

He was still asleep when she woke on Monday morning, so she showered and had breakfast as quietly as possible, tucked the five clearest photos into her purse, and slipped out the door.

At 7:30 am she pulled into a spot near Jeffrey's building. She knew that he often went in to work early, but she hoped that she would catch him at home. She did not want a scene at his place of work. For the first time it occurred to her to wonder if that woman would be with him? That might really complicate matters.

But it had to be done. Unbuckling her seatbelt, she grabbed her purse and got out. She tried not to think out exactly what she would say; she just hoped he'd be there. The thought of having to get back into her car and wait who-knew-how long didn't appeal to her at all. Too impatient for the elevator, she thundered up the stairs. But when she reached Jeffrey's floor, she leaned back against the wall and waited until her breathing was again even—she didn't want to sound breathless, which he might construe as nervousness and attribute to weakness. She didn't want him to call her bluff.

After ringing the bell, she listened intently for any sound from the inside. The pounding of her heart made this a difficult task, and she was thankful that Jeffrey would not be able to hear her internal organs. Outwardly she could play it cool, but inwardly there was no way she could stop the hammering. As she considered what she would do if he wasn't home—where she would find a restroom before settling in the car for what could be a very long wait—she heard the click of the bolt lock and the door swung open.

"Tamara! Is everything okay? Where's Mark?"

Tamara tried to push aside her guilt at scaring Jeffrey this way, and focus on the task at hand. He was standing in his bathrobe with Vi at his side, her tail wagging ferociously. Considering his circumstances, a widower with two adult kids suffering from severe polycystic kidney disease, she had to admit that he looked calm and at peace. *Must be the bimbo*, she though bitterly, even as thoughts that he deserved a life of his own flitted through her mind.

Ignoring Vi's happy greeting, she pushed her way inside, and turned to confront him. "No, everything is *not* okay! Mark is sick with polycystic kidney disease and his father refuses to donate a kidney to him."

Jeffrey sighed. "Tamara, we've had this discussion. Eric is a lot sicker than Mark, and could die now if he doesn't get a transplant."

"So you say. But between us, that's bullshit. No normal parent refuses to help a loving son in order to help another son who never spends a single second thinking of–"

"I'm not going to change my mind. I have to donate my kidney to Eric this week or he'll die. There's time for Mark to find a potential donor. We need to live day by day right now."

Having anticipated this, Tamara moved into phase two. "Jeffrey, I see that reason isn't going to make you change your mind, so unfortunately I am going to have to resort to doing something I'd rather not."

"What are you talking about?"

Taking a deep breath, she pulled the photos–enlarged and sharply detailed courtesy of Photoshop–out of her handbag. One by one, she placed them squarely on the table facing Jeffrey.

His eyes opened wide, then narrowed in confusion. "What... ? Who took these?"

"Aren't they lovely? I think the entire NIH personnel roster would enjoy seeing you with this bimbo. Don't you?"

Jeffrey took a step back, baffled and hurt. "You've been spying on me... and you are going to... blackmail me?"

"Bingo."

"But... "

"Mark needs your kidney. And if you can't do what's right for the right reason, then do what's right for the wrong reason." She picked up one of the photos and waved it at him. "I don't think that you being seen with *her* will enhance your career."

Jeffrey struggled to keep his cool. "Tamara, I understand your pain and unwillingness to accept my decision. I'm not even sure myself why I'm doing... what I'm doing. All I know is, whenever I think about *not* doing it... I can't imagine living with myself. If I let my own son die... I don't expect it to make sense to you. But this ridiculous attempt to blackmail me... I think you should just go home, and let's forget this ever happened."

"You'd like that, wouldn't you!" She raised her voice and began gathering up the photos. "Think I'm bluffing? Try me. I'll have these photos distributed so fast it'll make your head spin. I wonder how the administration will look at you–two sick sons and you out with some cheap whore."

No sooner had the words come out than Jeffrey's bedroom door opened and out came the woman dressed in what Tamara assumed was Mark's mother's bathrobe.

"Hi," she said, "I'm the whore. My friends call me Nina."

Tamara stared at her, unable to speak. The woman was very pretty, but wore no makeup, no fingernail polish, and no flashy jewelry. And she had an elegance that didn't fit Tamara's vision of how a prostitute would conduct herself. "I don't talk to whores," she finally said.

"Tamara, this is Dr. Nina Kaufman, Chief of the Adult Psychiatry Branch at NIH," Jeffrey said. He even chuckled. "Feel free to distribute your photos. I'm honored to be with her, and it'll only enhance my status if people see us together."

Chapter Fourteen

Mark retched again into the toilet, and when the nausea subsided, he stood, brushed his teeth, and turned on the shower. After several minutes under the hot water, he finally began to feel as though the world wasn't coming to an end. At least not quite yet.

As he was toweling himself off, he heard his cell phone buzz by the sink. He suspected it was Tamara, who had left the apartment, but as she was not scheduled to work this morning, he had no clue where she had gone. *Probably wants to chew me out for getting drunk. And then after that, she can chew me out for letting Dad make his own decisions about what to do with his kidney.*

But when he checked the number, he didn't recognize it. "Hello?"

"Mark?"

"Yes." The voice sounded familiar but he couldn't place it. "Who is this?" And then just like that, he knew. Shutting the seat on the toilet, he sat, suddenly too weak to stand up. "Eric," he said.

"Yeah, hey."

"Hey. Um... wow... so, how are you feeling?"

"You really want to know?"

"I really do."

"Everything hurts like hell. I don't know if I can stand this dialysis any longer."

This is what I'll be like in a few months, Mark thought, so full of dread that he felt like vomiting again. "Well, don't worry. You'll get Dad's kidney, and you'll be good as new." He couldn't keep the bitterness out of his voice, and added, "You've got some nerve, you know that? Making Dad feel like he owes you! After the way you treated him—"

There was silence on the other end of the line, and for a split second, Mark thought that Eric had ended the call. But then Eric said quietly, "Mark, can we talk?"

"Isn't that what we're doing?"

"No. Yes—I mean, we are, but I'd like to talk to you in person. It's really important to me. Would you come out here to the hospital?"

I have nothing to say to you, Mark wanted to shout. *I'm going to die because of you!* But something swept through him, some emotion... a regret so deep he felt an ache in his heart. His brother, his only brother, was dying. *First Mom, now Eric. Christ!* Memories triggered by the sound of Eric's voice bombarded him: Saturday mornings, squeezed together on the same recliner in the den watching cartoons (a ritual they continued until fourth or fifth grade), playing catch in the backyard, learning together how to ride a bike without their training wheels, all the dumb kid stuff they used to laugh at. And in that moment he thought he understood his father's inability to turn his back on his dying son. "What's the room number?" he asked, and wrote it down; then he texted Tamara and explained. And then he shut off his phone so that if she called it would go straight to voice mail. He couldn't talk to her right now.

When Mark stepped out of the elevator and headed down the hall, nausea rose. What was it about hospital cooking that smelled so disgusting? He understood the need for bland food—they weren't going to serve chicken biryani or curries here—but his mother had also made relatively bland, boiled chicken and vegetables, and it always smelled and tasted good. Giving up this line of thought with a shake of his head, he followed the signs to the dialysis unit.

Entering slowly, he didn't know what to expect. It had been years since he had seen his brother; not since he'd gone to prison. So he was shocked at the sight of the rumpled, unshaven, broken man with the graying hair and yellowish-gray pallor of an octogenarian. His identical twin, the brother who shared 100% of his DNA, was hooked up to a myriad of machines and monitors. He looked like he was withering away. He looked more dead than alive.

For a moment, Mark considered just turning around and leaving. Eric's eyes were closed, and he hadn't heard his brother come in. *I can't do this. I shouldn't have to deal with this.* But his feet felt glued to the floor. Pity swept through him, replacing all the anger. *No wonder Dad is willing to do whatever it takes to save him.*

Now his feet moved toward the bed, and he sat and stared. Eric's face looked so... not human... like a bad makeup artist had painted him yellow. And when Eric's eyes opened slowly and focused on him, it took everything he had not to get up and run out.

"You're here," Eric said in a weak, raspy, hollow voice.

"Yeah. I never thought we'd talk again."

"Life's fulla surprises, ain't it."

"Yeah."

"You good-for-nothing asshole!" exploded Tamara from the doorway. "You worthless human being... you should be back in jail for what you're doing here! Stealing my husband's opportunity to be a father and a scientist!"

"Tamara," Mark stammered. "Wait—"

"Shut up, Mark! I'm sick of you being such a..." she gestured, as if there were no words for how bad he'd been. To Eric she said, "How can you possibly think that you deserve your father's kidney more than Mark? What's the matter with you?"

Eric started to cough, and looked desperately at a cup of water on the table next to him. Mark picked it up and directed the straw into Eric's mouth. He took a sip, then pulled his head away and Mark put the cup back down. "The reason I asked Mark to come see me was because—"

"Well I won't let you do this! You hear me?" She came over to his bed and put her face practically in his. "You can bully Jeffrey and Mark, but not me!"

"I'm not trying to bully anyone," Eric said, and his voice was even weaker than before. "I want to explain."

"Oh, sure, *explain*. That'll relieve the guilt. Just tell him why you deserve your dad's kidney... you've been such a model son and upstanding citizen."

Eric lacked the strength to repel Tamara's outbursts, so he didn't even try; he just waited out her tirade finally said, "I *don't* deserve my dad's kidney. I'm telling you, really, I don't deserve it at all. But what am I supposed to do, off myself?"

"Yes," Tamara said. "Yes, do that."

"Tamara," Mark said.

"Okay, so if you don't deserve Jeffrey's kidney donation, then tell your father. Right now! Here's my phone, I'll call him."

Eric shut his eyes. "I already told him."

Tamara stopped shouting. "You told him... what?"

"That I don't deserve the kidney. Even if Mark didn't need it, I still wouldn't deserve it."

Relief broke out on her face, and Mark felt himself let out a huge sigh. At the same time, they reached for each other's hand. "Thank Goodness! So that means—"

"No," Eric interrupted. "When I told Dad to give the kidney to Mark, he refused."

Tamara felt as if she'd been hit with a block of cement. "No," she said. "You're lying. You haven't told him... he didn't say that."

Mark felt like something exploded in his head; the pain was so bad, he winced. *Wasn't that just like Dad, thinking he's doing the right thing.* The relief of a moment ago vanished.

"Nothing I said did any good. He said he made up his mind and he's not going to change it."

"Damn it! What the hell! Why is he doing this?" Tamara stamped her feet.

Mark shook his head; he had no answer. It was one thing if Eric had begged him to save his life. But for his father to insist on giving Eric the kidney... still, he couldn't keep from saying, "Tamara, he has made a strategic decision that he can save Eric, and that with a matched kidney for me over the next six to twelve months, both our lives might be saved. Isn't that what any father would do?"

"No! A real father would donate the kidney to his *real* son."

Mark, wondering why no nurse was coming in to find out what the shouting was about, heard himself say, "That's the real meaning of parental love for a child—to continue to support and love one's children is what parenthood is all about."

Tamara turned on him. "You know, Mark, your parents aptly named you—you're an easy 'mark.' You spend your whole life being considerate, generous, the perfect son, then your low-life brother shows up and inherits the one thing you need from your father. It makes me sick to see what a passive loser you are." She shrugged.

"I give up. Go back to being Mr. Goody-goody, and please thank your father for giving you the death penalty."

She turned and stormed out. Mark and Eric watched her in silence, and then looked at each other.

"So that's the little woman, eh?" Eric smiled. But he wasn't being nasty, he was trying to make Mark smile; the way he used to when they were kids. Before they had turned on each other.

Chapter Fifteen

Sitting alone at his kitchen table on Monday evening, Jeffrey felt overwhelmed by everything that had to be done by Wednesday. Knowing that he didn't even have time to think about how little time there was made him feel a little frantic inside. One thing was for sure–Jai had been on his case all week, and he could no longer delay calling Danfield.

Jeffrey Googled Robert Danfield and quickly found his office number at UCSF. Let's see, he thought, a three hour time difference–at 5:00 pm Danfield was likely still at work. His hands were shaking as he tapped the numbers on his phone.

"Hello?"

The voice was gruff and did not sound particularly pleased to have answered the phone. It's only going to get worse, Jeffrey thought.

"Is this Robert Danfield?"

"Speaking–who is this?"

Taking a deep breath, "This is Jeffrey Coleman. Do you have a few minutes?"

"Coleman," said Danfield. "I didn't expect to hear from you."

"Life is full of surprises." Without niceties or even a *How're ya doin?* Jeffrey was all business. "I just thought it might be good to clear the air, as it were, and maybe outline for you some of the directions my lab is taking. You see, I wouldn't want us to end up working on the very same angles and competing."

Danfield was quiet for a moment. Then he said, "I'm not really too worried–you know, we've been collecting a lot of data recently."

To Jeffrey that sounded like a challenge, but he maintained his cool. "That's good. Let's just make sure we're not both barking up the same tree. I'll tell you exactly what *we're* doing, and you can see for yourself. No secrets on our side."

"How generous of you," said Danfield, a snide tone having crept into his voice. "But to be honest, I really doubt that your group has the expertise to take you into the new areas that we're working on." His voice lowered suddenly, as though someone might be listening in to the conversation. "We've got some phenomenal new data–I envision a couple of very high-tier publications soon."

Jeffrey was losing his patience with Danfield, but did his best to mask it. After all, with what he and Jai were cooking up, Danfield would soon be reduced to groveling. He said, "Listen, here is what we've done recently."

Jeffrey unfolded a fascinating story, entailing all of the new data that Alok had picked up from the louse installed on Danfield's computer, cobbled together with a lots of his own pretend data– data that had been especially made up to continue the thrust of Danfield's experiments and take them to the next level. His delivery was flawless, outlining exactly what Danfield had already done, but adding complimentary studies and studies that Danfield would surely be planning to do. Jeffrey thought that if someone had called him and informed him that his lab had just done all of the things that Jeffrey's lab was in the process of achieving, he would have either passed out or sunk immediately into a deep depression. Or retired. When he finished the narrative, without being interrupted even once by Danfield, he put the icing on the cake. "So we're angling to submit these as two back-to-back studies to *Cell*," he said, naming one of the most prestigious journals–one that most researchers would donate their left testicle–or an equivalent female anatomy part–to get their papers published in. "What do you think," he said cheerily, but without waiting for an answer continued. "If they don't go through, I thought of talking to the editor at *EMBO Journal*–they might be interested."

Jeffrey sat back. His pitch was done, and all he could do now was to see if Danfield took the bait. But why wouldn't he? He had no reason in the world to suspect that there was a mole–or a louse– selling him out.

When there was no response, Jeffrey said, "Are you still there, Rob?" He purposefully used his informal nickname.

Finally, Danfield stammered, "Yeahhh, Cole–man. That's uh, uh, very–yeah very, uh. Interesting. Uh, yeah."

Jeffrey played the innocent Samaritan. "Do you think so? Thanks, Rob. Your opinion means a lot to us. It's great that you think our studies are interesting, especially since you are such an expert in the field."

Danfield was starting to pull himself together. "You know Coleman, a lot of the data that you have is very similar to data that we have obtained. Remarkably similar." Jeffrey could almost see the wheels turning in Danfield's brain. "I was uh, just uh, wondering."

"Yes?" Jeffrey replied.

"Well," Danfield fumbled on. "Uh, you know, given that we have so many things in common. So many similar experiments. Perhaps, uh, well, uh, maybe we can collaborate?"

Jeffrey could see that not only had he hooked Danfield, but he now had the opportunity to reel him in. "Collaborate? We love to collaborate." Jeffrey hushed his voice. "But, well, we're very close to submitting these manuscripts." That was a blunt lie, but essential to the overall plan.

Danfield seemed to be getting desperate, as though someone had pulled the rug out from under his feet. "But we can help you make the manuscripts even stronger. More data–a better shot at getting them accepted to *Cell*. We'd make a super team."

Jeffrey said, "Hmm," and pretended to think about it. "Tell you what," he said. "I have this little problem with getting my current manuscript on the mitochondria accepted." He laughed gaily, and then continued. "It seems as though one of the three reviewers is really trying to block our manuscript from getting accepted. You know, someone really petty." He stopped and let Danfield digest the information. "So while I would love to collaborate with you on those newer studies, I feel that I first need to concentrate on getting my initial paper accepted."

Jeffrey could almost hear the silence, and he envisioned Danfield sweating profusely in his San Francisco office. But he did not let up. "I'll tell you what–once this paper is finally accepted, I'll consider holding back on the newer work, and we can talk about collaborating and moving ahead. But for now, I need to focus on that one."

Danfield said quietly, "Okay. Uh, let me know when that, um... and then we'll work on the other."

"Sounds good! I'll be in touch!"

"It worked!" Jeffrey told Jai a minute later.

"Alok's louse saved the day!"

"Yes, Jai, but let's forget all about that now—no more mention of Alok and the louse. Your main goal now is to move ahead with the newer projects—if Danfield finds out that we don't really have a lot of that data, we're cooked."

"Got it. I'll get to work right away."

Jeffrey greeted the boy at the door. "Hi, Jamie."

"Hi, Dr. Coleman."

"Thanks for coming by." Jeffrey watched as Vi sprang up to greet Jamie, and was pleased when he sat on the kitchen floor and let her lick him as he hugged her. "I'm glad she's so comfortable with you."

"Yeah, we're cool. Mom said you wanted me to come over and walk her three times a day, plus feed her in the morning and the evening."

"Yes. I'll leave a check for you. And, er, Jamie... there's something else I want to ask you."

"What?"

"When someone has surgery, there's always a possibility of complications. If anything should happen... If I don't... well, if there's a problem or something... here's my son Mark's phone number. Could you please have your mom call him and let him know? And ask her if he'll take Vi? He's the one who got her for me, so I'm sure he'll be willing to take her."

"You're going to be fine, Dr. Coleman," Jamie said with the carefree confidence of the young.

Jeffrey watched him rub Vi's head until she slumped into his lap and rolled over so he could scratch her belly. "Just fine," he repeated.

He spent the rest of that day and the next in feverish activity; planning and making sure that nothing would be forgotten. He spent several hours in the lab, talking to all of his personnel, and ensured that Jai's paper was ready for submission and that Jai would be able to take care of that on his own. He talked with his lawyer, and his accountant, checked his will, and organized his finances. Finally, he took a deep breath, sat down and wrote out four very long and difficult hand-written letters to Mark, Eric, Nina and a final one explaining the situation to his lawyer. He addressed the envelopes, attached postage and his return label, and set them aside. They were to be mailed the next morning, on the way to the hospital; he must not forget.

Jeffrey's last errand that evening was a meeting with Ravi at the Starbucks. He hated Starbucks, much preferring his own strong Italian espresso maker, but he didn't want to trouble Ravi to come to his apartment, and he didn't have the stomach to go over to Ravi's place, where he would undoubtedly be forced to exchange pleasantries with his family.

They sat across a small table from each other, ensconced in leather armchairs and holding cappuccinos. There was light music, and the nearest customers were well out of hearing range. Jeffrey didn't waste any time–in fact, he didn't have much time left. "Do you have it?"

Ravi tapped his single-strap shoulder bag. "Right here. Sodium pentothal." He looked up at Jeffrey. "Listen, I'm not here to lecture you, but–"

"Then don't, Ravi," Jeffrey interjected. "My mind is made up. You know what I'm doing and why–and you yourself said you would've done the same thing in my position."

"Jeffrey." Ravi shook his head. "I would be irresponsible as a physician and as a human if I didn't force you to think about this one more time." He took a sip of his cappuccino. "I have to ask you to reconsider."

"Ravi, you know my sons. Well, you know Mark, anyway. I have no other choice. This is the only thing I can do to ensure they both stay alive. Before we go through the details one last time... you're sure the drug won't affect my kidneys?"

Ravi looked pained. "The kidneys will be fine."

"Okay. Let's go through the plan again."

It was fairly straightforward, and Ravi, whose specialty was nephrology, was familiar with the protocol: Jeffrey would be admitted to the kidney transplant unit the next morning. As soon as everything was ready, he would be taken for the pre-operation prep about an hour before the scheduled surgery at 11 am. Just before being wheeled out of his room for the prep–and this was key–Ravi would come to his room and provide him with the reconstituted vial of sodium pentothal. To avoid potential legal issues and ensure that Ravi would never feel legally or morally responsible, Jeffrey had decided that although Ravi would provide the drug, he himself would administer it through the IV. This shouldn't be difficult; the IV would already be hooked up to the back of his hand, and all he would have to do would be to align his syringe and push the plunger into his IV drip. This dose of sodium pentothal had already been used to kill several death row inmates. Underneath his hospital gown, Jeffrey planned to wear a chain that held a letter enclosed in a page protector, essentially admitting his suicide so that both of his kidneys could be donated, with one to each son.

Jeffrey also knew that the only potential flaw in the plan was Mark. Eric was already in the hospital, but Mark was not; he wasn't even prepared for the possibility of receiving a kidney, he wouldn't have fasted or avoided taking aspirin products. But that's probably how it was with all transplants; recipients needed to be ready with just a couple of hour's notice. And since Mark was in the DC area, he'd be able to get to the hospital quickly.

But rather than leave anything to chance, he'd decided to email them and explain that there was a serious possibility that Eric might die–even with the transplant, and that Mark should be ready on the chance that the kidney could go to him instead.

"So, I guess that's it," Jeffrey said. He rose and extended his hand to Ravi. "Thank you."

Ravi pulled him into a hug. "I can't believe I am having to do this for my friend," he said, and his voice shook. "I'm a doctor, and I'm helping a healthy person die."

"You're saving two lives for one," Jeffrey reminded him. "You're doing the right thing, Ravi. And I... thank you."

Ravi didn't answer. He just held Jeffrey for a moment longer, then, with head bowed, left quickly.

At the Chowdhury home, Ravi sat across the table from his wife, Lakshmi sipping tea. The kids had been excused, and had gone up to their rooms to do their schoolwork. "Ravi, what's wrong? You just seem so melancholy this evening. Is it a patient at the hospital?"

"Yes," Ravi lied. "A patient." Then he slammed down his mug of tea and cursed.

Lakshmi's eyes widened in fear. "Ravi, what is it? You must tell me! This is not just sadness for losing a patient—I know you too well."

Ravi exhaled slowly, and then took a huge breath. "You're right, Lakshmi. It's, well, much worse. But I really shouldn't say— I've been sworn to secrecy."

"Ravi! You know you can trust me. I'd never give away any confidential information."

"You promise you won't be critical of me?"

"Who, me?" She smiled. But when Ravi did not smile back, she said, "I'm sorry, Ravi. Of course I will support you. With whatever is troubling you."

When he explained, she protested, "Ravi, that's illegal! Assisted suicide is not allowed in this country! They could take your license away—or put you in jail!"

Ravi's forehead creased. "I know it's illegal. Officially. But it's done all the time in hospitals and hospices."

"This is not the same thing as pulling the plug on a respirator, or asking that extra measures not be taken to keep a terminally ill person alive. He's a healthy person!"

Ravi sat down again. "I know," he said. "But I understand him. I mean, wouldn't you do the same thing if it would save the lives of our kids?"

Lakshmi was so scared for him that she had to fight tears. "Yes, yes. But Ravi, please don't get caught. I couldn't survive without you."

He took her hand. "I won't. It'll be okay. Really, I promise."

Later that evening, Jeffrey sat on the couch, gently stroking Vi's head. She had, in that magical way of dogs, picked up on Jeffrey's melancholy. Rather than racing around the apartment trying to get Jeffrey to take her out to play, or even play tennis ball fetch in the apartment, she was gentle and passive. She knew something was up.

Jeffrey would have liked to have a glass of wine or a beer, or six beers, but that was out of the question. He wasn't going to do anything that might endanger the kidney harvest, or interfere with his plan to donate both kidneys. No, his life would end without another glass of wine or beer. Or chocolate. Or ice cream. Or ahi tuna steak. Without seeing the Himalayas. Or Alaska. Or his grandchild. The list was endless. Until this evening he never really realized how little he had traveled, and how badly he wanted to see and do things. After Annie died he should have taken the boys to Patagonia or the Dolomites. Well, that wouldn't have happened because Eric had been in jail. But he could have taken Mark. Except both he and Mark had been so wrapped up in work. Missed opportunities.

He pushed Vi aside, and went to get his laptop. Vi was always offended whenever he had to break off a session with her on the couch—even just to answer his phone. So rather than sit at the table, he grabbed the Macbook and settled back on the sofa. Vi bounded on top of him, her head firmly ensconced in his lap. Gently pushing her head aside until he could free the keyboard, he began working on the letter to his sons. It took him close to two hours to get the phrasing right, but he finally felt satisfied that he had correctly explained the situation. Two hours, he thought grimly; about twenty percent of his time remaining on this earth.

Dear Eric and Mark, or Mark and Eric: I took a considerable amount of my (remaining) time to figure out how to best start this letter. Despite what one or both of you might think, as a father, I love you both, and want only the best for each of you. This is not the time for affixing blame, so I am not going to go into the problems or difficulties that we have had – me with each of you in the past, or right now, in the present. It's meaningless. What's important is that you understand that everything I have done and am now about to do is for **both** of you. Yes, **both** of you.

From the moment I realized that you were both ill with Polycystic Kidney Disease, my life has been a nightmare. There is no worse scenario for a father – for any parent – than not being able to help your own flesh and blood. With one exception: being able to help one son but not the other – one son **at the expense of the other**.

Many years ago there was a movie called *Sophie's Choice* about a Polish mother who was forced to decide which of her two children would be sent to death in the Nazi gas chambers, and which child sent to forced labor, with at least a chance of survival. That is how I have felt, having to make such a difficult decision. But then I realized that, unlike Sophie, I have **another choice**. Not one or the other, but a creative solution. (Whoever said that scientists aren't creative – well he didn't know what he was talking about!)

I have two kidneys, not one. You each need a kidney to survive. So do I – but unlike Sophie, by relinquishing my own life, under the right circumstances – such as a car accident – you could each receive one. However, trying to choreograph a car accident in which the driver (me) dies without causing injuries to his internal organs or any other drivers or pedestrians, proved to be impossible.

So I have arranged a relatively painless and straightforward way to end my life and allow for you both to have a kidney, and hopefully go on to lead long, happy and productive lives. I have taken steps to ensure that I will die peacefully tomorrow morning in the hospital before the kidney harvest. "Tomorrow morning" is a dated statement. Because I have asked Ravi to forward this email to each of you from his iPhone shortly before I execute this plan. I do not want you to try to stop me, and by the time you receive this it will be too late.

Am I afraid to die? Hell yes! It wasn't in my calendar. As a scientist, I know that there is no afterlife, that your mom will not be waiting for me at the end of a rainbow, in some white dress with wings. We live once, and like the rest of the animal kingdom, we die. Our bodies decompose, and our individual atoms spread among the rest of the living earth. I read once that every living human (and non human) today has atoms that once made up part of Shakespeare's body. So in a sense, we live on, our atoms reshaped into other living beings, endlessly. And more specifically, I will live on through you, my kidneys attached to your bodies.

All I ask is that you both live your lives well, honestly, truthfully, fairly, fully, and hopefully, also happily. And I want you to have some sort of a relationship with each other, as brothers. I will leave it to you to decide how, but that is of crucial importance to me.

My time is now running out. I don't intend to sleep tonight, my last night on this earth, but rather to look at photos and albums, watch videos of our family, when you were kids, listen to music and sort through some of my things. Being tired tomorrow may make things a little less painful for me.

In a few days, via Ravi and my lawyer, you will each receive copies of my will and instructions regarding my estate. Everything is in order, and it will not be a burden. You will split my savings and estate, but there will be no life insurance to collect – as they will rule my death a suicide, and that will negate my policy. However, a kidney is obviously worth more than money can buy.

With that, I send you both my love as a father. I wish we could have all gotten along better in recent years, as a family. I wish many things, but now I'll have to be satisfied with just wishing you each a long and healthy, and happy life, and that you remember always how much both your mother and I loved you.

Dad

Jeffrey's hands were shaking as he clicked the *send* button on his laptop, and his carefully-crafted letter to his sons made its way to its transitory station—Ravi's inbox.

Sitting down with a pile of photo albums in front of him, he sipped water and thought how wonderful it tasted. Simple tap water, chlorine and all. It never tasted so good. And here he was—supposed to fast from midnight on—he would never drink water again. *It's remarkable how imminent death sharpens the senses and forces one to appreciate all the things we take for granted,* he thought. *Almost a pity we can't experience some near-death experience early on in life, so we never forget how valuable living is.*

Jeffrey flipped through the albums. Photos of Annie with the twins at her breast, just after they'd been born. One of Jeffrey struggling on the carpet to change both their diapers at the same time. That had been a riot—getting hit in the face with a full stream from Mark. Or had it been Eric? They had both been active babies. As he leafed through the pages, he thought he heard a knock at the door. He climbed off the sofa, with Vi leading the way to the door. Unafraid of burglary or murder, he pulled the door open without bothering to look through the peep-hole. In the doorway stood Tamara.

He dreaded another fight with her; especially tonight! but said, "Hi, come in if you want, but I've explained my rationale to you, and you don't seem to accept it. At this point, I don't know if there's really much more we can talk about."

"Well, you're wrong. Until now, I've tried to reason with you politely. But this is your last chance."

"Please go home. Be with Mark. He needs you. And I bet your baby would be happier if you got some rest."

"Here's the deal, Jeffrey," she said in an ice-cold voice, "if you don't save your kidney for Mark, I promise you—I swear to you, you'll never see that grandchild of yours. Never. Not once. I will make sure of it."

"I understand. I do. And I know that you are only trying to do what you think is best for Mark. All I can say is that I appreciate it, and I understand your frustration with me. I hope that one day you'll forgive me.

"Forgive you? Why should I forgive you? I mean this! You'll never see this unborn grandchild. Never! Not even once. Unless you stop this stupidity and do what's right for Mark!"

"Tamara, I accept your decision. But what can I do?" he shrugged; wished he had not let her in.

"I hate you!" she shouted. "You are the worst father a son could have!" With that, she stormed out, slamming the door behind her.

Jeffrey sat and wrestled with conflicting emotions: while he could understand Tamara's anger, he felt angry too—at her for trying to bully him. *My last night on earth and I have to listen to her scream at me*, he thought; then, *In her defense, she doesn't know it's my last night*. Would it make a difference if she knew? He thought about how she was going to feel when it was all over. Her threats, her hurtful parting words. He felt sorry for her, then. Would she tell Mark about tonight's visit? Or would she live with the shame in silence? A memory came to him, of the first time Mark brought Tamara home. As usual, Mark had been ill at ease, shy, and needy of his parents' approval. Tamara, on the other hand, had walked in as though she owned the place. "Mark, take my coat, will you?" and turning to Annie, she had smiled and said, "Mind if we turn the thermostat up? It's freezing in here."

Annie had immediately taken to her, instinctively realizing that she was right for Mark—that her sassiness and down-to-earth practicality was exactly what he needed. Someone to light a fire under his abstract-thinking butt. But Jeffrey had not been so sure. Sure, she was loyal and definitely a fighter, but there was something underhanded about her, like a boxer who illegally kicks or hits below the belt. He knew right away that he wouldn't want to get on her bad side.

Later, he had said to Annie, "What do you think?"

Annie, in her typical good-natured way, had put her arm around him and said, "I think Mark has finally found someone who will be good for him."

"Are you sure?" Jeffrey had asked. "I mean, it's just that she's a little, well, I don't know. The image I have is of a middle linebacker."

Annie had laughed. "I'm not into football analogies, but I gather that means she can look out for his best interests." She had hugged him again. "Mark my words—no pun intended." Annie had loved puns. "She'll be great for him."

Jeffrey smiled glumly at the memories, and then recalled Eric bringing home a girl. Inked up in a jean-jacket with piercings wherever he looked, and probably in places he couldn't see and didn't want to look. Annie sighed as they pulled up in front of the house, but had been pleasant to the girl when they came in. Jeffrey had had a harder time controlling his temper, knowing that Eric's primary goal was to rattle them. When they sat down in the sunroom and Annie asked if they wanted coffee or tea, the girl, whose name Eric had not yet divulged, said, "How 'bout a beer?" Jeffrey said, "No," but Annie had been more polite: "I'm afraid we don't have any in the 'fridge, but if you'd like something cold, we have lemonade and ice water." Eric's answer was, "No she doesn't want lemonade—what do you think, that we're two-year olds?" Then he grabbed the girl's sleeve, pulled her to her feet, and dragged her out of the house. Jeffrey had been furious, but Annie just smiled and said, "He just needs to find his own way. That's part of the process, showing his independence and lack of need for our approval."

Taking a deep breath and giving into tears, Jeffrey tried to empty his mind and get some sleep. But he was still awake when the alarm sounded at 4:00 am. He slid out of bed, trying not to disturb Vi. *Hey, it's still dark out,* her eyes seemed to say as she watched him without raising her head. The pain Jeffrey felt as their eyes met and he realized he would never see her again was so deep and so harsh that for the briefest of moments he considered calling off his plan.

But no. With a heavy sigh, he brushed his teeth without swallowing any water as per the doctor's instructions, and sat down in front of his laptop. Now gratitude swept through him: he'd had a fascinating and successful career and over the years had mentored many students who had gone on to become notable scientists in their own right.

He was hopeful that his two sons would be healthy, and that Mark and Tamara would forgive him.

Then his thoughts turned to Nina. The last time she called he claimed to be too busy to see her, and he could hear the hurt in her voice. *I can come over there, if you would rather, and we can eat in,* she'd suggested. How would she react? Would she be furious? Would she go to The Barking Dog and get drunk on Chardonay? Would she cry? Come to his funeral? Talk to Mark? After Mark's embarrassing visit, he couldn't imagine it. She'd be in pain, that he knew. But as much as he hated with all his might what he was going to do, he felt that he had no choice. So he composed another email, to Nina, and explained his plans. He ended:

> Please don't hate me for all eternity. Of all the things that I need to do before showing up at the hospital later this morning, know that this is the very hardest. I never thought that I would be anything but alone for the rest of my life – with the exception of Vi, of course. But then you came along, and suddenly everything changed. Never in my life did I imagine that I'd "pick up" such a potentially important part of my life in a bar—but there you are—life is full of surprises.

Nina, in the short time since we have met, I have come to love you. My greatest regret in not living out my natural life is that I will miss the opportunity of developing a new future with you. I can't express how much that hurts—every time I think about it—but it's extremely painful.

As the tears are starting to dribble down onto my keyboard, I am attaching a recent photo of me – and Vi – I wish I could take a photo of you with me, but it won't help where I am going.

I wish you a wonderful life—think of me once in a while, but don't mourn me—I am doing what I need to do. The only thing I can do. And remember—I love you.

Jeffrey

As he tapped the *send* button and watched the message and photo go, he set down the laptop, fed Vi the remaining treats from her container, stroked her short fur and hugged her, grabbed his bag and headed out the door. It was only 5:30 am and he wasn't supposed to be at the hospital until 7:00 am, but who wants to sit in DC traffic for their last morning on earth?

Chapter Sixteen

After the anesthesiologist had conferred with Jeffrey, said, *See you soon!* and left the room, Jeffrey lay in his bed in the kidney transplant section at Georgetown Hospital, and listened nervously to the pounding of his heart. Nurses were coming in and out of the room, taking vitals, asking questions, and obtaining signatures. But where the hell was Ravi? Jeffrey didn't know exactly how long it would be until they wheeled him out for pre-op, but he guessed it would be within the next hour or two. If Ravi didn't arrive in time, they would harvest only one kidney... never again would he get this chance... and the emails! They would be sent out, and Mark and Tamara would immediately come to the hospital for Mark's surgery... Jeffrey's stomach twisted with nerves; so anxious now that he felt nauseated. He took deep breaths and tried to calm down. *If I don't die as planned, Tamara will surely kill me.*

A male nurse stood across the room, fiddling with some equipment. *What if they take me early? Dammit! Where is Ravi! This isn't like him to be late. Has he changed his mind?* Starting to feel the bile rise in his throat, Jeffrey slid his cell phone off the nightstand, powered it up, and speed-dialed Ravi's number; he heard Ravi's ring, Vivaldi's *Four Seasons*, "Summer Concerto," but not via his phone; it came from the pocket of the male nurse, who quickly pulled out his phone and muted it. He turned to face Jeffrey, and despite the black glasses and thick moustache, Jeffrey recognized him. Relief spread through him. Ravi glanced at the door, and then stepped up close to Jeffrey. "I've been here for over an hour, but there are nurses everywhere. *Real* nurses. I couldn't get near you without raising suspicions. I will stay away until just when you're ready."

"Thank you Ravi," whispered Jeffrey, turning off his phone for what he knew would be the very last time. "I'm ready."

At the same time, Mark was sitting across from Tamara at their little kitchen table, sipping coffee and eating cereal with milk. "I keep thinking that I should be there, you know, to encourage Dad."

"Encourage him to give your kidney away to someone else?"

He understood her anger, but her voice could be so ugly sometimes. "You know, it's possible that I might still get a kidney from someone else. I still have time. You shouldn't be so hard on Dad."

"Yeah, and it's also possible that you *won't* get a kidney. Ever. And that your dad's decision may lead to your premature death before your first child is even born."

"I think we need to look at it differently; from Dad's angle. He's looking at the big picture, and making the calculation that's best for both Eric and me. I mean, if I were in his position, I would probably come to the same conclusion."

Tamara couldn't even look at him. *He doesn't get it. He's one of the smartest people I know, and yet he doesn't get this at all.* "He's playing percentages with your life, Mark. With all of our lives: yours, mine, and the baby's. It's one thing to do what he can for Eric, but at the expense of *you* potentially dying? And what if there is no kidney for you? What then? He's choosing to save Eric and gambling that you'll live."

"But Eric is going to die *now* if he doesn't get that kidney. By 'now,' I mean today, tomorrow, next week or the following week. It's imminent. What do you expect Dad to do? Eric is his son too."

"Eric gave up his right as a son long ago with his behavior. Your dad should show his loyalty first and foremost to you." She checked the time on her cell phone. "And they're probably wheeling him into the operating room right now." Just then the phone rang. "My dad," she said.

Wonder what he would have done, Mark couldn't help thinking, as he watched Tamara click on. To his surprise, her face lit up, there was no other way to describe it, as though the sun had risen through her skin.

"Are you serious? When? Oh my God, Yes! We can be there! Thanks! Bye!" She hung up and said, "Mark! My dad got you a kidney!"

Mark sat and waited for what she said to make sense, and when she said, "We have to go!" he said, "Wait. What?"

"My dad serves on the hospital advisory board for the University of Virginia Health System, and he has been quietly trying to help out. This morning he looked at your file and he says they have a kidney for you. Right now!"

"Now?"

"Yes! We have to make arrangements and head to Charlottesville. Mark, he said that the kidney is a much better match than your dad's!"

It took a moment for the news to sink in, and then he was on his feet, grabbing his keys. "I'll be back as soon as I can."

"What? Where are you going? We need to leave now! We have to get to Charlottesville!"

"I have to let Dad know," Mark said, sliding the strap of his backpack over his left shoulder. "I know it sounds crazy to you, but... I just need to let him know that I'm going to be okay. That he made the right decision. If I leave right now I might be able to get a message to him before they put him under." Without waiting for her to respond, he hurried out.

Feeling light as air, he was making good time as he headed south down Wisconsin Ave. toward Georgetown Hospital, cutting in and out of lanes, and tearing through every yellow-to-red light. But when he turned west onto Reservoir Road, only mere minutes from the Georgetown Hospital parking lot, traffic slowed and then came to a grinding halt. There was a pickup truck in front of him in his lane, and a big Chevy Suburban monster ahead of him in the lane next to him, so he couldn't even see what was going on ten yards ahead. But from the wails of ambulances and flashing blue lights in the distance, he knew that there must have been a bad accident. This wasn't just a slow-down due to excessive rubbernecking; it was a situation in progress, and he was stuck with cars in front and behind, with nowhere to go.

"Damn, not now! Not now!"

The driver of the car next to him stepped out and tried to see around the enormous SUV blocking the view in front of him. Mark opened his window. "Can you tell what's going on?"

"Looks bad. Someone up ahead with *WAZE* wrote that there are fatalities. We're stuck here for a long time, I'm afraid."

I won't get to see Dad, was his first thought; then *I have to go get a kidney!* Frantic, he tried calling, but it went right to voicemail. *Too late, he must already be in surgery.* Sadness washed through him. "I should have gone in with him," he said out loud, hitting his steering wheel with the palm of his hand. "I should have been there for him." But then he thought, *I'll just have to see him afterwards, after we're both done with our surgeries. I know Tamara said she never wants to see him again, but I do.*

Inching his way to a side street, he swung in and headed back home. Then he remembered that his father's friend Ravi worked at the NIH clinical center—and he was a nephrologist. He might know someone on the ward at Georgetown; maybe he'd even be able to get a message to him.

With his back to Jeffrey, and anyone else who might come into the room, Ravi flicked the syringe to remove any remaining air bubbles. Tears filled his eyes, then ran down his cheeks, and he didn't turn to face a nurse who came in and checked Jeffrey's vitals for the last time. "We're just about ready for you," she smiled.

"Thanks," Jeffrey said, his eyes on Ravi's back. When the nurse left, Ravi went right up to him.

"Jeffrey," he said, "it's still not too late to change the plan. Suppose there is a donor in two weeks—your death will have been in vain."

"Suppose there's not," Jeffrey sighed. "I can't have this conversation again, Ravi. This is the only choice I have."

Ravi bowed his head, didn't bother to hide the tears. "Okay, it's ready, Jeffrey. Take it." Making sure that they were still alone in the room, he slid the stand with the IV hookup closer to the bed. Pointing to the bag of saline that was dripping slowly into Jeffrey's arm, he said, "All you have to do is open here—then just slide the needle in and push the fluid from the syringe into the bag."

"Okay."

"I have to go. Hopefully no one will notice me on any of the security cameras, and with your letters, no one will even think of looking for an accomplice. But I've got to get some distance between me and this place before the shit hits the fan." He clasped Jeffrey's free hand with his. "I'll look out for Mark. And Eric. Go in peace, and know that I will always think of you as my friend." With that, Ravi turned and passed through the door.

Ravi was shaking and struggling to hold himself together as he approached the elevator and hit the button to go down. No sooner had he done so when Vivaldi piped up on his phone again. Sliding it out of his pocket he didn't recognize the number. He looked around worriedly, and then answered quietly. "Hello?"

"Dr. Ravi Chowdhury?"

His gut tightened. *Could they have found out already?* "Yes, who is this?"

"It's Mark Coleman, Jeffrey's son. I was on my way to see my dad at Georgetown, and I'm stuck in this awful traffic jam on Reservoir Road. I need you to get a message to him, is that possible?"

"What, uh, what message?"

"Please tell him that a donor has been found for me! A much better match than Dad. I'm going to have the surgery today!"

As the elevator doors slid open, Ravi spun around and ran as fast as he could back to the pre-op. "I have to call you back, Mark!" he shouted. *Please let me get there on time!*

Bursting into the room he saw a whirlwind of activity surrounding Jeffrey's bed. "Stop!" he yelled. "Disconnect the IV!"

The nurses in the room stopped and stared. But Ravi didn't slow down—he yanked the bag of saline off the stand and off the IV line. Jeffrey was so shocked that he couldn't speak at first. "Ravi...? What are you doing?"

"Jeffrey, did you... "

Jeffrey stared, shocked and betrayed. "I don't know what you're talking about," he said, looking at the nurses. "He probably shouldn't be here."

"Mark called! They found a kidney for him!"

"*What?* Who?"

"I have no idea! But it's a good match, Jeffrey—he's having the surgery today!"

"Sir, we have to ask you to leave," one of the nurses said nervously.

"I will," Ravi promised earnestly. "Jeffrey, give me back the…"

"It's right here," Jeffrey said, taking it out from under his hospital johnny. "And the note, take that too!"

"What is going on here?" thundered another one of the nurses, an older woman whose name-stitched smock identified her as Marge.

Ravi and Jeffrey had forgotten they weren't alone, and Ravi froze, the syringe in his hand.

"Give that to me," Marge instructed, holding out her hand. "And tell me what is going on." At the same time she unclipped a device from her waist and said, "I need security right now in room 604. This is an emergency."

"This is all a misunderstanding," Jeffrey said. "Ravi is an old friend of mine. I swear. It's okay."

"No, it is *not* okay! What's in the syringe?"

Just then, two burly-looking hospital security guards entered the room. Marge pointed at Ravi. "Please escort this gentleman, who is *not* a nurse on our staff, to the visitors conference room and wait with him until I decide whether to call the police."

"Yes ma'am," said the older guard, putting a giant paw on the shoulder of a shaken Ravi. Jeffrey shouted, "Wait!"

The guards stopped and the older man turned his head toward Marge. She nodded slightly, and the guards waited. "Well?" she demanded.

"This is Dr. Ravi Chowdhury–he is a nephrologist and a good friend of mine."

She looked at Ravi, scrutinizing him carefully. "You're a doctor?"

"Yes. I work at the NIH."

"So what's this?" she asked again.

Jeffrey answered immediately. "It's mine. It has nothing to do with Ravi. He just came to visit me. To cheer me up. I'll explain about the syringe, but please let him go. He probably has patients waiting."

Ravi blinked several times, but was unable to speak. Marge thought for a moment, and then turned to the security guards.

"Please escort the doctor off the premises. There are no visiting hours now."

Ravi looked hopeful that a crisis had been averted, and sent a smile at Jeffrey. "I'll see you when you get out of surgery," he said.

"Yes," Jeffrey nodded. Suddenly it hit him, what had just happened. Mark had a kidney! He was going to be just fine! "Yes, I'll see you, Ravi."

Ravi was happy to leave, despite the security people following close on his heels.

Marge turned her attention back to Jeffrey. "Start talking. And it better be good."

"It is," Jeffrey assured her. Patiently told her the whole story, from the discovery that Mark was ill and the search for Eric as a potential donor and finding that he was already hospitalized, right on through the entire plan to commit suicide and donate both kidneys. The only thing he left out was any reference to Ravi and the support that the latter had provided in carrying out the plan.

She shook her head, and actually smiled. "Well, that's a new one!" She patted his shoulder. "I should probably report you for attempted suicide. But you know what, I would've done the same thing in your position." Now she laughed. "If I had been smart enough to think of it!"

Jeffrey laughed too.

"So here's what I'm going to do. I'm going to take this syringe," she tapped it lightly, "and get rid of it. Are you okay with that?"

"More than okay. Thank you!"

Epilog (one year later)

As Jeffrey opened the door, Vi leapt in the air, thrilled at seeing Mark. "Vi, down—no jumping," said Jeffrey, worried that she would knock Tamara over, along with the baby in her arms. Then he said, "Come on in."

Tamara came in and gave Jeffrey a long hug, careful not to squeeze the baby that she held to her shoulder. She was no longer angry with Jeffrey; on the contrary, she was ashamed of the way she'd acted, and still had a hard time looking him in the eye, despite the fact that Jeffrey had told her he didn't bear any hard feelings.

"Dad, this is a really nice little cottage," Mark said. "Looks like you're all settled in."

"Come on out back," Jeffrey said, "I'll take you for a tour later. Nina is barbecuing the turkey."

"Barbecuing?" Mark said. "Turkey? Never heard of that."

"Me either. But trust me, it'll be great."

Jeffrey slid open the patio door and Nina waved from the grill. "Happy Thanksgiving," she greeted Mark and Tamara.

"Happy Thanksgiving." Tamara, in particular, had grown surprisingly close to Nina, and gave her a warm hug.

A tall muscular man who was comfortably parked in a lawn chair got up and walked over to the group. Jeffrey said, "Oh, Mark, Tamara—let me introduce you to Darren Townsend. He's the detective who located Eric on Randolph Road. And the guy who saved his life when the two gangbangers came to the hospital to hurt Eric."

Mark shook his hand warmly, "Great to meet you! Dad told me so much about the way you took on those two guys in the hospital—you really saved his life!"

"Thanks Mark—but you know, I don't think I saved his life. They would've abducted him and then knocked him around a little, scared him up. But if they actually killed him, they'd never have gotten their money back."

"You did save his life, Darren," said Jeffrey. "Even if they only planned to injure him and threaten, he was in such bad shape that any physical violence would've likely killed him. That's what the doctors say."

Darren took a slug of his beer, and smiled shyly. "Right. Whatever."

Mark cracked a beer of his own and sat down. "Is he really coming, Dad?"

"He said he would. Whether he actually does or not is anyone's guess."

"I hope he does. I want him to feel like... like he's part of the family. I want him to get to know his nephew."

"I do too," Tamara surprised them by saying.

Just then, the doorbell rang, and a silence spread over the gathering. But before everyone could tense up any further, Ravi and Lakshmi came through the gate at the side of the house.

"Ravi, Lakshmi, over here!" Jeffrey called.

Ravi shook hands with the Coleman men, and exchanged hugs with Nina and Tamara. Lakshmi took Jeffrey aside. "You know, I could've killed you myself for the risk you made Ravi take."

Jeffrey grimaced. "I'm really sorry, Lakshmi. I didn't intend to put him at any risk. I thought that everything had been completely foolproof—I didn't know who else to turn to."

Her face softened. "I know, Jeffrey. I understand—as Ravi put it, we each would've done the same for our own children." She then moved her left foot forward and punched Jeffrey hard on the shoulder. "Now we're even," she said. "Sometimes it's necessary to carry out a symbolic revenge in order to be ready to forgive."

"Symbolic," Jeffrey repeated, wincing and kneading his bruised shoulder. But he was smiling.

The doorbell rang again, and Jeffrey trotted inside. He didn't come out immediately, but when he did, Eric was right behind him.

Tamara looked at Eric and did a double-take. She whispered to Mark, "Is that really him?" because now that he was healthy, clean, and in decent clothes, he looked completely different.

Eric grinned. "Yeah. Mark got the brains, but I got the looks."

That broke the ice. Amid smiles, Jeffrey introduced Eric to Darren—although they had met briefly at the hospital, Eric had not been in a state of mind to meet and greet. "So you're the gumshoe who saved my life?"

Darren shook his hand. "I'm just glad to see that you're doing well, mate. Gives me a real sense of satisfaction."

"Well thanks, man. You are a pro."

Darren bowed slightly, but for once did not reply.

Eric was introduced to Ravi and Lakshmi, and then to Nina, who said she hoped he was good and hungry.

Finally Jeffrey led Eric up to Tamara. Eric's gaze fell upon Jeremy, and he said, "Can I... ?"

Tamara glanced nervously at Mark, and held Jeremy more tightly to her chest.

"Come on, pass my nephew over," Eric said. "I'm clean. No alcohol or drugs, and I'm a committed uncle—seriously." He shrugged. "I can't explain it, but for some reason I really like kids."

"Jeremy," Mark said to his son, "say hello to your Uncle Eric." He reached out to take him from Tamara, but there was no need – she handed him over to Eric and said, "If he spits up on you, don't take it personally."

"People have done worse things to me," Eric said, and surprised everyone when a tender expression crossed over his face. "He looks like me when I was a baby," he said in a voice filled with wonder. "Just like me!"

"And me," Mark added.

"Are you two going to continue the twin brother competition *ad nauseum*?" Jeffrey asked, and the whole group laughed.

Eric circled the little yard, carefully holding his nephew, talking and cooing as he moved. When he finally rejoined the group, he returned Jeremy to his sister in law, and took out several envelopes.

"Here," he said, handing the first one to Darren. "Here's a retainer. I don't plan on getting into any more trouble, but just in case, I want you on my side."

Darren smiled, thanking him. He had enjoyed taking down those losers at the hospital, but it was always nice to receive a tip for a job well done. But he was too polite to peek inside and see what Eric had given him.

He handed the next one to Jeffrey. "Dad." Eric said, moving toward his farther with another outstretched envelope. "Here."

"Eric. This isn't necessary. Please."

"Dad," Eric insisted. "Take it. It's yours. It may not be necessary for you–you may not need the money. But I need to give it to you. It's everything I owe you over the last ten years, plus, well, interest."

"Eric, where did you get all this money from?" Jeffrey asked.

"Ah," said Eric. "Good question." He smiled brightly. "Remember those scum who tried to kill me–but thanks to Darren are now in jail via the hospital? Well, they claimed I owed them money."

"And you didn't?" asked Jeffrey.

"Sure I did. But only because they changed a deal we had and threatened to rat me out. So I hid the money, and then I ended up in jail. I managed to get a friend to move the money and hide it until I got out."

"So this is drug money?" Mark said.

"Money is money," said Eric. "But no, not from drugs. It was payment for depositing money in an account for them. But in any case, I made most of the money on the stock market."

Jeffrey stared. "You made this money on the stock market?"

"Yep. I invested some of the money I deposited, made more, and slowly kept investing." He made muscles with his arms. "Superman! I turned under $20,000 into nearly $200,000 over the last nine months. But now I want to complete a business degree and do things the right way."

Jeffrey shook his head slowly. "Thank you for this, Eric. I really appreciate you thinking about me. But I can't accept it. It just isn't right."

"Dad," Eric said. "You have to take it. You have been saving my life over and over. You literally gave yours up for mine. For ours." He looked pointedly as Mark. "I owe it to you—you have to accept."

Jeffrey shook his head again. "I can't." But then he brightened. "Wait. Eric—you are really serious about parting with this money?"

"I am."

"Then I'll donate my share to the American Cancer Society. For research and helping people who died so young, like your mom."

"What a wonderful idea," Nina said, looking with admiration at Jeffrey.

"Typical Dad," Eric smiled. Then he handed the final envelope to Tamara. "Here—I didn't have time to pick out a card, but this is something to start Jeremy's college fund. Open it!"

Doing as she was told, Tamara slid the envelope open to find a stack of one hundred dollar bills. Gasping, she said, "How much is here?"

Eric waived her off. "No biggie. Just ten grand for my favorite nephew. Did I mention that Jeremy is my favorite nephew?"

"Eric," began Mark, but Eric cut him off. "For once, you listen to me. That's a present from his uncle. Put it in a nice safe account and leave it alone for eighteen years. No arguments."

"But," interjected Mark, "we can't accept that. Like Dad said, it isn't right. Maybe we can donate it to the American Cancer Society, too."

Tamara stepped forward with Jeremy. "Mark!" she barked. "Who made you the spokesperson for our family?" She turned to Eric. "Thank you, Eric. We'll be delighted to accept this on behalf of Jeremy and his future education. After all, you are Jeremy's favorite uncle!"

Jeffrey smiled, noting that Tamara was true to her form. Always looking out for her family. She was a real survivor, he thought, with all of her senses honed and zeroed in on looking out for her husband—and her young son. Good for her! "This calls for a toast," he declared. Raising his beer, he said, "To health, happiness..." and looking directly at Eric, he added, "and family."

They sat down together at a large green plastic table in the shade of the back yard. Nina brought a steaming tray of barbecued turkey over to the table and placed it in the middle. "No worries,

Ravi and Lakshmi—I've got tons and tons of grilled veggies and lots of vegetarian options." She turned to Vi, who was sitting by Jeffrey's side at the table, studiously watching the proceedings, and ready to intervene should any scrap of food fall—accidentally or not—in her direction. "No worries for you, either, Vi—there'll be tons of turkey left over!" Then turning to the twin brothers, she said, "Your dad tells me that you were both great meat eaters—that you even used to have competitions when you were kids about who could eat the most."

"I always won," said Eric. "But I never told anyone that I'd get really sick afterward." He smiled at his brother. "It was worth it, just to beat you at anything."

"I just figured that you'd be much bigger than me, because you always ate twice as much," said Mark.

"Yeah, the grass is always greener… " said Eric.

Nina poured herself a glass of wine. "Well, let's just have a really friendly competition today. No winning or losing. But lots of eating and drinking."

"Sounds great to me," said Eric.

Mark said, "Man, for a long time I couldn't eat at all… when I was so sick. But since the surgery, I've gotten my appetite back." He patted his belly. "And how! But – " he added, "there's one dish that I absolutely won't touch."

"What?" asked Jeffrey.

"Kidney pie." Eric grinned, and they all laughed.

Jeffrey held up his hand. "I feel the same way, Son."

About the Author

Dr. Steve Caplan is a Professor of Biochemistry and Molecular Biology at the University of Nebraska Medical Center in Omaha, Nebraska. He has won a number of prestigious awards for his research and mentorship and his laboratory is supported by the National Institutes of Health. Dr. Caplan teaches graduate and medical students, and mentors his own group of Ph.D. students and post-doctoral fellows. He is the author of numerous peer reviewed scientific papers, as well as several published short stories. He also blogs on *Occam's Typewriter* and *The Guardian's* science page. His first novel, *Matter Over Mind*, received positive reviews and reached the Amazon Breakthrough Novel Award quarterfinals (top 5%). He has since published *Welcome Home, Sir*, and *A Degree of Betrayal*. *Saving One* is his fourth novel.

www.ingramcontent.com/pod-product-compliance
Lightning Source LLC
Chambersburg PA
CBHW051304250626
47155CB00009B/3429